TOMORROW I'LL SAY, ENOUGH

TOMORROW I'LL SAY, ENOUGH

by Silvina Bullrich

translated by
Julia Shirek Smith

Latin American Literary Review Press
Pittsburgh, Pennsylvania
1996

The Latin American Literary Review Press publishes Spanish language creative writing under the series title *Discoveries*, and critical works under the series title *Explorations.*

Library of Congress Cataloging-in-Publication Data

Bullrich, Silvina, 1915-

[Mañana digo basta. English]

Tomorrow I'll say, Enough / by Silvina Bullrich: translated by Julia Shirek Smith.

p. cm. -- (Discoveries)

ISBN 0-9035480-70-3

I. Smith, Julia Shirek. II. Title. III. Series.

PQ7797.B75M313 1996

863--dc20 95-21098

CIP

The paper used in this publication meets the minimum requirements of the American National Standard for Permanence of Paper for Printed Library Materials Z39.48.1984 ∞

LATIN AMERICAN LITERARY REVIEW PRESS

PITTSBURGH, PA

Acknowledgments

This project is supported in part by a grant from the National Endowment for the Arts in Washington D.C., a federal agency, and the Commonwealth of Pennsylvania Council on the Arts.

I dedicate this book to the Oriental Republic of Uruguay, land of my grandmother, a generous and hospitable land.

S. B.

The characters in this novel are fictional. Any resemblance they might have to real people is mere coincidence. The places are imaginary also, more or less inspired by what I saw during a few hours spent in La Paloma and by the map which painter Giovanni Gazzo has kindly drawn for my benefit.

S. B.

December 19

My first impulse had been to put the clocks away in a dresser drawer and for a hundred and twenty days not even be aware of the time. Wasn't that my plan, my heroic decision, the only way I could save myself? Perhaps, but I didn't feel capable of carrying it out so rigidly. Everyone knows that plans, budgets, and fidelity always allow a margin for error, the possibility of minor deviations which do not add up to betrayal.

In the meantime my old alarm, an Omega with a dirty, worn leather case, went off in its usual subdued manner. I had chosen an arbitrary time, 10 or 11 a.m., a normal, ordinary time, suited to the habits of my previous life, just right for knowing I wasn't waking up at 3 p.m. or at sunrise. Fine and good, so now I know it's ten and I can go on sleeping. I can go on sleeping until eleven or twelve or even until April 5 when I have to be in Colonia at 4 p.m. to board the car ferry for the return trip to Buenos Aires. But, except for instances of hibernation, no one can sleep one hundred and twenty days, and those days have to be filled up somehow.

I dozed a while longer, then realized it would be better to face reality: I was on vacation. No one needed me. When I went to bed, I hadn't left on the night table any little notes about urgent business. Nothing, a blank day, more than one hundred and ten blank days remaining. Still, among all these days without event there was one very important for me: my birthday. Today, precisely today, December nineteenth, I have reached forty-nine. No one has thought ahead to the possibility of a woman's someday reaching forty-nine and the years beyond. All those years beyond, before old age and death, but which no longer exactly belong to life. Next year

I'll turn fifty, that fatal number.

In previous years I had spent my summer holidays like *everyone else*, in a place where *everyone else* spends the summer holidays. I went to Mar del Plata for more than three decades, and I still remember the old boardwalk, the destruction of which seemed to us an act of heresy. Once I went to spend *Carnaval* in Río. Out in the street I became frightened and claustrophobic, and it seemed as if I would never, never be able to free myself from those dense walls of sweaty flesh, that I would go down to my death beneath the sky and the tinsel. As for going to Europe, in the dead of winter I don't always do so, because it's difficult, which means I deprive myself of itineraries and inns and the anticipation of arrival. And then, for ten seasons I went to Punta del Este, like *everyone else.* Until one day I said, "Enough!", and I'm writing this to explain why I said, "Enough!" and why I find myself alone in a seaside resort with the romantic name La Paloma, where along vast beaches and a sea with its pristine blue intact there is nothing which could even be called a village.

I did not come here with a friend—male or female—with a lover, nor with a relative. I came alone because I detest being alone. I fear solitude, and I feel it always crouching close by in some corner or other, like a silent, poisonous toad. I know my life is in its power, that it can kill me when it decides to do so; but amid the emptiness which being forty-nine signifies for a Latin woman, I suddenly felt it essential to consider why life unfailingly leads us, with a gentle but firm hand, to a stage when we are superfluous on the earth. Something similar must have occurred at our birth. "A girl," the doctor, the midwife, and the father were exclaiming in resigned tones. "Ah, well, the next one will be a boy." I wonder if someone out of pity for my infinitesimal perception said, "Maybe this girl will become another Madame Curie, or do as much for humanity as Florence Nightingale, or perhaps be a great artist.... On the other hand, a boy might have been born—a possible pimp, cardsharp, or simply a dolt like the ones who make up that modern demimonde called café society." No, I don't think anyone has thought or said such things. The male carries on the family name, although that name may be as common as Perez or García, and there are so many others to carry it on. The male.... But let's leave males aside. I owe them many moments, good and bad, and I assume that throughout these days on my desert isle I'll have time to remember men and to examine which one of them contributed much more to humanity by being born than did I by being born humbly and unwittingly with female parts.

For the moment, I must leap out of bed, open the windows, and begin the day. A bare minimum of activity is more powerful than my solitude. I wash my face, brush my teeth, put on faded old terry cloth coveralls (once orange or yellow, I think, and now almost white), slip on a pair of espadrilles, go to the kitchen, get the empty water jug and go fetch fresh water for tea. In Punta del Este too I would go fetch water, at Stop 8, but I would usually say hello to someone I knew, and the kids hanging around the faucets would fill my container and put it in the car. I go alone here, on foot, slowly. I don't say hello to anyone, and I come back to my romantic white cottage, where the windows overlook the rocks.

One by one I perform the everyday movements. I arrange the tray with cup, saucer, spoon, saccharine (of course I don't use sugar). I pour boiled milk into a small pitcher, slice bread. The toast browns while the cup of water I poured into the kettle comes to a boil. Butter? Not a good idea, but one has to be allowed some treats—all the more so today, my forty-ninth birthday.

While I eat breakfast, I'm remembering the boy I met in the water yesterday. He was swimming in the same lazy, awkward way I was, and he smiled at me. I smiled back, sadly. It's a shame I do not really like young men, the only ones always available; furthermore, my being shut away in that cottage which seems uprooted from some Greek island—Mykonos, perhaps—probably seemed to him very romantic. At least that's what I thought I detected from the few words we exchanged after stepping out of the water.

"Cold, isn't it?"

"Yes, but once you're in, you don't feel it."

"I live over there," he told me, pointing to a modern house, tasteless and undoubtedly comfortable, and which could barely be seen from the beach.

I realized that was his way of asking me where I lived. Inwardly, I thanked him. These were the first words I had exchanged with anyone for several days, other than sales people and waiters. And I still had one hundred and ten days to go.

"You're living in the white house above the rocks, aren't you?"

I felt flattered. With that blind confidence we all have in the miraculous, in the possibility of an encounter (yet another one!), and in the future (although almost our entire life may be over), for an instant I believed he had been looking at me, observing me, following me since my arrival. The thought occurred to me that perhaps by making an effort I could become interested in a man much younger than I. At least create an amorous friendship, confused and ambiguous feelings, something which would be like a triumphal shout in my ear: "Don't you see that you did well in coming to this solitary place, that destiny awaits us when we least expect it, just as death came to the gardener of Samarkand?" "Don't you see that while avoiding the humiliation endured by lone women in Punta del Este, the futile phone calls, and all that undignified behavior of someone who rebels against the inevitable, you have at least managed to have a young man look at you as if you were a goddess?"

"How do you know where I live?" I asked him almost coquettishly although, fortunately, I emphasized the "almost."

"I'm Nino, Luigi's son. Yesterday I served you white wine and clams."

Curtain. No comment.

However, to myself I comment on all of it. If he hadn't been Nino, the son of Luigi the café owner, would his smile have altered my solitary state? That segregation, that implacable segregation by class, race and sex, which explains why I am here influences me as strongly as it does those who rule Latin nations. Yes, I know—a black man became a city official in New York, there are several women judges, and what is happening to me no longer concerns anyone since it is not occurring in the present generation nor will it in those to come. Of course, that's what they told Jews after the (supposedly) last pogrom. In the United States, girls from good families marry working-class men and in Sweden.... And how does that concern me, if I don't live in the United States and have never set foot in Sweden? Here, in this Latin land, the café owner's son smiled at a mature woman because she was a customer in his father's café. Never would his intentions be otherwise. If he were a lunatic or an angel, and if he could pass through those barriers which are as impassible as all irrational and traditional obstacles, it happens I cannot do so. I have a very clear idea of my social position, my financial status, and my age. I know perfectly well who my parents were, my four grandparents, my eight great-grandparents, and my sixteen great-great grandparents. There in the family vault are our name and a date in the distant past. We have one of the first vaults in the Recoleta. Nor, once dead, are we left in peace. On November 1 and 2, when the departed are remembered, people passing by the marble wall covered with memorial plaques comment on whether we have flowers or whether we are among the forgotten, godforsaken dead even though perhaps one or another of us may be in Heaven.

"How is business?" I asked him, the one who was to have been the affirmation for my insanity—that is, my solitude in La Paloma.

"Mm...not bad."

"But there aren't many people."

"Well, the season starts after Epiphany."

The same trite phrases uttered in every seaside resort, and I couldn't blame Nino since it was my fault. The stupid questions had been asked by me. Why? To hear a human voice a little longer.

Yes, I know the first thing I should explain here is why someone who detests solitude chose for a long summer stay at the most solitary spot on the Uruguayan coast. I could answer that it is because of La Paloma's beauty, but I would be lying. I am here because I need to know in a precise way something which, to tell the truth, I do know in a precise way: a Latin woman not compelled to earn her living can disappear from the world for as long as she pleases without its occurring to anyone, anyone at all, that this woman—young still, full of energy, initiative, and enthusiasm for work—might be fulfilling a useful function in a realm where a great number of useless men are pretending to do so. No, I'm not referring exclusively to Latin America. I'm thinking also of Spain, Portugal, Italy, France. For us women the centuries have not gone by. The same destiny predicted for us when we were born and when we married is reserved for us in maturity: family life, dedication to children and grandchildren. Such interesting conversations! Such exchange of ideas! Always the same, at the same table...then, a word of protest, the right to make a fuss. But, Dear Lord, I chose another destiny. I sacrificed my youth. I have a career. I have a name. Those thirty years of uninterrupted work cannot have gone by in vain. Fine, no one is stopping you. You may have talent. What? Come now, you heard me—paint, write.

All the time, you mean? One book after another? One painting followed by another? Exactly. That's inhuman. Many men who struggled as I did obtained posts which allow them a decent living and a sense of fulfilling a mission while they await the birth of the theme for another book or for the picture they will never paint. But you are not a man. I know that, but I am a human being. All right, that's what the world is like. The same thing happens to black people, to Jews from time to time. A worker is not a boss. Classes and races do exist. You, Madame, cannot obliterate them. But I belong to that class from which come consuls, ambassadors, cultural attachés, directors of directorates. But they are men. But I have worked like a man. But you are not a man. And what am I supposed to do? I don't know. It's sad you don't enjoy taking your grandson on the merry-go-round. I'm not talking about enjoying myself, I'm talking about fulfilling a mission, holding a position which is right for me. No, I don't like merry-go-rounds or little horsies or any other diminutive. I will give my grandchildren a name they can take pride in.... Leave that to the men. And what is there for the women? Merry-go-rounds.

I rouse myself, pushing my breakfast tray aside. I take my mattress and my bag, and I head for the beach. I cannot keep debating obstinately and repetitively with an invisible interlocutor who has 300 million mouths. As insistent as I may be, he won't say I ought to close up *La Barcaza* (that's the name of the cottage) and return to Buenos Aires because the world needs me. No one needs me except perhaps Luigi and Nino. Thanks to the white wine and clams they'll serve me, they'll be able to convince themselves that the season isn't so bad and that there are indeed some tourists.

I prefer to create my own emptiness rather than submit to the emptiness created by others. Emptiness and solitude are two phantoms dwelling in every human being but in Argentineans especially. Maybe I should say in people from the Río Plata since I notice the same phenomenon in Uruguay. Everyone crowds together at La Brava, leaving vast stretches of sand and sea lonely and deserted, to be used by a privileged, extravagant few. Sometimes, even in Punta del Este, I have found myself alone out in the sea. I have looked to my left, to my right, behind, ahead—no one. It would make me almost afraid and at the same time gave me a marvelous sensation of power. On one such morning I became aware that even were it just for one summer in my life I ought to seek out solitude, immerse myself in it, entangle myself in its clutches. One has to have willpower, I told myself. Everyone utters this kind of nonsense, as if one could decide to have willpower without having it already. One has to be nice looking, one has to be young, one has to be rich, one has to be a winner—these are the watchwords of the times, and to be all those things of course one has to have willpower. But to decide to have it merely for a reason as old-fashioned and outmoded as finding oneself turns out to be much harder. All the same, I managed and here I am.

December 21

I went outdoors almost unconsciously, climbed slowly down

to the rocks, walked between them cautiously, and sat down on the flattest one. My fingers searched eagerly in the shallow pools of stagnant water until the terrified little crabs, about as big as my thumbnail, began to come out. One, two, three, ten, eleven—many came out, and I was delighted. I was feeling life around me. Life, I cannot live without feeling life constantly, like oxygen. There are clams too, but they do not create a sensation of life. And there is open water which can hardly be considered alive, viscous and with no more movement than that imparted by the waves. And there are sharks. They say these beaches are infested with sharks and that it is not wise for me to stray far offshore. For the moment I have only established a relationship with the crabs hidden among the rocks. That started the day before yesterday, and I'm already heading toward them as if toward an assignation.

I stop and change direction—an assignation with crabs, me! I who have.... All right, I swore to myself to avoid all lying and all exaggeration. The men in my life weren't such important people. None of them aspired to conquer space, none of them.... I am lying again. Maybe I am simply forgetting. I am a forty-nine-year-old South American woman, so I can hardly have been the grand passion of the kings of the international deck. But my life was rich, and is rich, since no one can rob me of those memories, those palpitating realities.

Now this time, this summer, I have planned only one thing: to isolate myself in order not to be a woman alone. My father would have shrugged his shoulders, declaring there was nothing clever in my paradoxes. And I would have kept quiet, devouring my inward vow to be more important than he supposed I could ever turn out to be. I was the one who was right. It is not a paradox. I simply have to come up with what is, for me, the definition of a woman "alone," in the sad, fragile sense of that word. If instead of coming to La Paloma I had gone to Punta del Este, I would be a woman alone like so many others. I would be trying to do what I could with my hair, which would be damp from sea water seeping in despite a good bathing cap and at the same time dried out from the sun, that relentless South American sun. I would put on.... No, before putting on anything I would look over my closet carefully, and I would review the possible dress of the other women invited to the same cocktail party.... I would ask Gilda, Patricia, and Florencia what they intended to wear. Gilda is a good person and never intentionally lies, but she changes her mind every few minutes; therefore, I shouldn't go by her reply. Patricia lies on purpose. Assuring me sweetly she will have on a certain item, possibly the same long cocktail dress she wore last Saturday or a blouse signed by the illustrious marquis, at the last minute she would show up looking radiant in a garment she never mentioned nor acknowledged having in her wardrobe. Florencia has so much personality that her reply is no kind of guarantee. She wears her clothes better than anyone else, and I worse than anyone else. Three futile telephone calls. If I call Jeannette or María Clara, it will be the same. I know them—either they lie or change their minds at the last minute. I should manage such things alone. How complicated! I detest fruitless struggles as much as I detest fruitless investments. I don't enjoy competing with elegant women nor purchasing gold ingots. Both these activities produce in me the same sensation of cold. The world becomes harsh and hostile, turning into an immense shipwreck where each individual clings to the fragile objects which still appear to be afloat.

"What could you be thinking about that you won't even say hello?" The voice of Humberto, the tavern keeper who paints, snatched me from my meditations. What a shame! I was just about to find the thread of my interior labyrinth. But I have so much time ahead of me!

"Hi, Humberto. I didn't see you."

"Right, I know that. I, on the other hand, don't have to see you. I divine your presence. I came to the doorway as if I knew you'd be passing by."

Bravo! This man seems to be courting me, but only when I'm passing by, and the rest of the day is long. Extremely long. If I come to The Magic Seashell every night I will end up going to bed with him. Of course, the trouble is that I enjoy less and less going to bed and making love. In the past I would wear flowered panties which seemed to fly off me of their own accord. Nowadays my panty girdle forces me to make awkward movements, and in my partner's effort to help me pull it off I sense a grave dread that something may come apart. But nothing comes apart. It's not worth fussing over, but he went through the fear and I the bother. Furthermore, cultivating loveless love has never appealed to me. It's not my thing, it bores me as much as playing bridge, and it's not possible to leave in the middle of the game

"Don't you want to come in? I spent five hours painting yesterday. I was feeling inspired...."

I too was feeling quite inspired when he interrupted me. I wanted to remember exactly why it terrified me so to be a woman alone at an elegant beach. To seek out someone to take her to dinner...to go to the area where her friends have their beach umbrellas set up.... No, impossible to give shape to my thoughts while Humberto goes on talking....

"It isn't either abstract or figurative. I'm creating the sensation of having painted a figurative landscape if you look at it from a distance, because the planes are softened as in any seascape; but up close you'll see they are abstractions; it's only color which allows me to create this sensation."

He is a rather appealing man. I don't like his little gray mustache, which contrasts with the hair just starting to turn gray; nor do I like those black glasses which he never takes off, as though he didn't want people to read his look.

"I imagine you take off your glasses when you paint," I say to him.

"Of course," he answers with a laugh. "Why do you ask? Do they bother you?"

"A lot."

"Ah!" I see him hesitate. Finally he takes them off. He suffers from a slight squint and his eyes are too close together, but his expression is pleasant. He looks at me as if begging for a favorable opinion.

"I like you better this way."

He laughs delightedly but puts the glasses back on. People have their idiosyncracies. One has to respect them.

Suddenly I realize his glasses would bother me less if they didn't make me think of my son-in-law. He is a nice young man, what Argentineans call *una monada*: that is, a little darling. He always steps aside when a lady is about to enter the elevator and even goes so far as to stay on until the floor above so he can return to his own pleased with his gallantry. "Come in, ma'am. Good morning, ma'am. How is your doggie doing? What did the vet say? I'm so happy to hear that. See you soon, ma'am." After all that he can kill, steal, and rape, and no one will resist him or believe he's really guilty.

How can a *monada* be guilty of anything? That's my older son-in-law. The other one, if we're distinguishing between them, has decided to adopt an attitude exactly the opposite. I'm mortified that he has spent a night in police custody for wearing his hair long, but I consider this a matter which should be settled between him, his wife, and his barber. I'll confine myself to not understanding very well what his hair has to do with the police.

Ah, how I envy barren women or those who resort to the pill. In my day we were able to resort to countless other means of avoiding reproduction, but I refused to do so until I had three children. I wanted two boys and a girl. I had three girls, and I grieved for a while. But ever since I've had sons-in-law, I've understood my good luck. Those two could have been my sons. My youngest daughter, Nickie, married three months ago. They send me predictable, defiant postcards. Behind the set phrase, "From here, in this magnificent city of Venice, we think of you with deepest affection," I read: "While you roast in Buenos Aires or stagnate alone in La Paloma, we are having a splendid trip." I was always noble enough not to send my friends postcards. Noble and also sincere, because behind those hackneyed colors, that unchanging pale blue sky, those waters hardly skimmed by a gondola, the illuminated Arch of Triumph with a French flag waving inside for Bastille Day, there lie countless other realities. Days of rain and melancholy, the stench from the canals of Venice, or the lack of accommodations, Florence flooded, the Plaza de Toros in Madrid when bullfight season is past, the argument between him and her over whether to take the metro or a taxi or stroll along the banks of the Seine when he knows perfectly well that her (in this case, Nickie's) feet are aching, and he (Facundo) can't speak a word of any foreign tongue.

No, the first of my Ten Commandments of Friendship is: "Thou shalt not send postcards to thy friends." When I had money I would bring them some gift, and when I didn't, I'd let them have the satisfaction of observing that every trip comes to an end and that after a while I, like them, have docilely allowed everyday life to take over.

I'm thinking all this while Humberto shows me his canvases, with their thick layers of paint and their muddy colors. He does not know how to prepare pigments nor how to apply them in the proper proportions; moreover, he does not feel happy until he disfigures his best creations.

I praise a small canvas in tones of gray and sky blue.

"It's going to turn out nicely, but it needs a few touches." Combining word and gesture, he splashes it with vermillion: "See, that way you notice it's a sunset." My opinion matters to him. He has read some of my art criticism. It's useless to argue. Maybe between now and March 31 I can convince him.

"I should be going now."

"No, not yet..." he begs.

He takes me by the shoulders, presses me against him, and wants to kiss me. Fine, let him kiss me. What do I have to lose? At least I'll gain time. He presses me harder and harder.... I don't need much intuition to realize nothing is happening. I pretend I'm defending myself against a satyr in rut: "No, please, I should go to the hotel. There is a message from María Clara...another day, Humberto...rather, another night."

He pretends to be understanding. I add some things about how I have to go to the market, how I have to buy mussels before only the worst ones are left. I regale him with arguments so he will assume I don't notice his momentary total incapacity to keep me there with a valid reason. He sighs—I have made him suffer, I am a cold woman, I don't understand his passion. I walk off apologizing. I don't know if woman is more likely to be the weaker sex, but at least when it comes to matters of intimacy her weaknesses are less pathetic than men's. I flee from him like a nymph forsaking King Pan.

While I head for the hotel, where I am indeed going in search of news—since as far as I know there's no other telephone around here—I am thinking that my successes have been less than mediocre but at least I am not to blame for anything. I did not seek out anyone. I came to be alone. I would like to write that on a sign and put it up over my threshold. It would be an infallible way of attracting a crowd at all times.

The hotel is across the way, up the hill on the other side of the only avenue deserving of the name. I look at the building, and distress overwhelms me. Of whom can I have news which will have any direct impact on me, which will serve to brighten up my day or make me dream tonight? I know, almost for certain, that Dolores and Iván are going to arrive for a visit at the end of this week or the beginning of next, with Alejandro, who at the age of six leads the life of an adult since they consider that the best way to love a child is to drag him with them everywhere. As a result my grandson is pale and skinny, with the sad gaze of an improvised adolescent. His large melancholy eyes often disappear under lids weighed down by drowsiness. With the instinct youngsters have, he senses that a strict schedule would agree with him: getting up early, taking naps, eating foods which contain vitamins rather than savoring the same dark-colored, carbonated drink whenever he feels like it. I know he would be grateful to me for a little strictness, but by now I am tired of taming children, and the best method would be to no avail if his parents were to abandon it forty-eight hours later. He will ask me for a Coke or a Pepsi and will be disappointed to see that I give it to him right away. Then he will keep his fingers around the glass for half an hour without taking a sip, until someone gets impatient and tells him to drink it or put it down on the table, that he's going to break the glass. Undoubtedly he will put it down, and his long, dark lashes will once more sweep his pale cheeks, while I, seemingly impassive, will implore Heaven to let me hold on to my patience and my feigned indifference so I will not interfere in the households of other people, even if they are my daughters. Let them call me an old egotist, but not an old busybody.

Old? So am I already old? My steps have strayed from the goal just set and are going back to carrying out their previous plan: I am on my way to buy provisions. This afternoon there will surely be time to stop by the hotel.

At the little store they receive me with their usual cordiality. They let me choose without forcing their products on me. Competition is non-existent. Before nightfall they will have sold their perishables, and if they have chosen to put down roots in La Paloma, it is because they like the peaceful life.

Doña María is a fat, smiling woman; Don Eleuterio is more talkative. He has told me he lived in Comodoro Rivadavia for several years, and he is as proud of this fact as some of my friends are of having lived in Paris. One has to recognize he knew the era of prosperity, the oil fever, the Yankees who used to arrive in "trailers" (he used the American term), those large collective suits of armor, instead of wearing individual suits of armor, but which under the sun shone just as bright and silvery. The dollar served as currency more often than did the modest peso, and on windy nights the women brought in from Buenos Aires would see arrive at the proliferating cabarets men who seemed to have stepped out of an old cowboy movie, with khaki pants, wide leather belts, green bills bearing a likeness of George Washington, men with an insatiable thirst for whiskey and for love. It was love, Don Eleuterio insists, real love. Many men divorced in order to marry our motherly prostitutes, who used to cook stews and bake cakes for them instead of simply resorting to the can opener.

His stories entertain me, and I buy an abundance of fruit, some cheese, ham, fresh vegetables, a chicken. I'll buy the mussels at the port. Eleuterio is sorry he can't offer me spider crabs, which they have in Comodoro. Do I like spider crabs? Of course. It's too bad there aren't any here. Yes, it's too bad. I say goodbye.

Suddenly I realize I'm cheating at the hermit game. I have come in search of solitude and a headlong confrontation with my deeper self, and I am turning into something like the mailman who stops to chat at every door. Will I have to admit that solitude and I make a terrible pair? Maybe human beings find serious obstacles to living in a cordial atmosphere free of complications and hostility. I am quite used to having to steel myself for attacks from the man who swears he adores me or from the daughters who consider themselves three examples of filial affection. In this serene world which gives me more than it asks of me I am withering like a plant without water. No one is telling me I am egotistical, vain, smug, too weak, or too strong. In that eternal battle which is life I am a forgotten soldier in a hamlet where no one will be going into battle. I think the troops stuck along the Maginot Line must have felt something similar throughout that year.

I must rouse myself. As a start, I return to the house almost running, empty my sack of provisions on the kitchen table, wrap the piece of Gruyère in a damp towel and put it in the refrigerator. I put the eggs in place in the oval egg-pockets inside the door, the butter on the top shelf, the fresh vegetables in the plastic container. Everything is in order. I close the refrigerator, go to my room, look for my beach bag. The bed is still unmade. The woman who comes to straighten up has neither a watch nor the slightest sense of time. She never arrives at the same hour, but it doesn't make much difference to me. I'd rather not run into her. I communicate through slips of paper on which I scrawl a few orders: "Change the sheets, take my pink and blue blouse to the laundry, iron my black pants, sew the missing button on my navy shift. I'll leave the button right here next to the paper." She always leaves some answer and from time to time, especially on rainy days, we run into each other and have a chat. Her history seems to be a blank canvas surrounded by a frame of family illnesses: her uncle suffers from dreadful back pains, her mother is going blind, her little girl has a racking cough, her sister is pregnant, and for fear that it's catching she is not going to visit her. The litany goes on, monotonous for the one hearing it, but intense and palpitating for the one living it.

December 22

The road shimmers under the burning one o'clock sun. I'm heading for the beach. I crave cool, salty water. A slight breeze, humid and tropical, won't let us forget we are near Brazil. I'm thinking that in Mar del Plata the air is cool and as brutal as a whip, that in Punta del Este the same breeze probably blows much cooler. But the important thing is that the sea is here. I have never figured out why we humans, generally speaking, are so drawn to the sea. The poems of Baudelaire are not enough of an explanation for me.

Santiago adored the sea. He was an excellent swimmer, and we used to make love in the water. It was terribly exciting and complicated. We were both excellent swimmers, and we would move off through the still waters of the Mar del Plata Yacht Club. We would get as far as some boat hidden behind a dinghy or solent, and he would kiss me passionately on the mouth. Young mouths, young kisses, fresh breath, saliva salty from sea water, and his fingers on my firm skin, on my solid and defiant body, and the grace of any kind of movement, even the most sluggish, of the unintentional duckings, of my soaked hair drawn back, of our two heads, blond and silky in spite of the salt. Ah, youth, I miss neither your torments nor your passions. I am only sorry that as you go off into the distance you leave behind you this fuzzy caricature of myself.

I arrive at the beach, and the task of getting out my beach umbrella and mattress distract me from my gloom. With the umbrella over my shoulder and my arms full, I walk slowly to the place where I am generally accustomed to setting up camp. I get settled and take from my straw bag the cream which gives me a tan without drying out the skin too much. I watch my actions as if I were someone else. All my gestures seem false and depressing. They all emphasize the forty-nine years I've just reached. Maybe bathing will allow me to shake off my black thoughts. I put on my swim cap. I can no longer allow myself to go around with my hair soaked and pulled back. But, I ask myself angrily, what the hell can a woman who is getting old allow herself to do? The water feels almost warm. It reminds me of Acapulco. Everything reminds me of something. I resemble a cash register of past events. "*Bon giorno, signora*!"

Nino is swimming next to me. I wonder if it's by chance that we run into each other in the middle of an immense sea, like neighbors on the same elevator? We swim in silence for a minute. Both of us want to show off. For a few moments I have the impression that we are a couple. Then I return to reality, stop and float. I put myself in my proper place, him in his: I ask if the season is off to a good start, if new vacationers have arrived, if there are a lot of mussels. He replies to everything with that made-to-order optimism which tradespeople in summer resorts have. Business may be good or bad, but they are determined not to allow vacationers to feel sorry for them. Besides, in the end every year is more or less the same. In countries where the summers are long, people can deprive themselves of everything except getting away for a summer vacation. Those who have exercised their willpower up to the end of January end up going away in February or even in March so they can tack their holiday on to Holy Week. We are coming out with all these trite phrases but behind them I feel we are really friends. He will always seek me out on the beach whether I go to eat mussels at The Merry Mussel or not. My black thoughts have faded a little on contact with the water and Nino's conversation. Now they're pearl gray. Now I have the courage to find out about the message in which Dolores will be announcing her arrival.

December 24

Iván, Dolores and Alejo arrived to spend Christmas with me of course. I never felt older than when I saw them get out of the car a couple of hours ago loaded down with packages just as we used to be when we went to the ranch (ex-ranch, now only empty land and a house) to visit my seventy-two-year-old grandmother. We would feel that we were nice, worthy of being characters in a third-grade reader. My daughter and son-in-law feel the same way. They have brought panettone, nougat, walnuts and hazelnuts—exactly what I bought yesterday—also great bunches of grapes, pretty little candles shaped like pine cones, a bottle of whiskey, and a princely gift: "a toiletry case for me who likes travelling so much," made of quite heavy leather and filled with little glass bottles.... I think the twenty kilos allowed me in tourist class would be completely swallowed up were I to carry on this treasure. I give them thank you hugs. I brought the gifts for them and for Alejandro from Buenos Aires. We'll put them all on the tree tonight: French perfume for Dolores, a Pierre Cardin tie for Iván and a pirate set for Alejo, besides some frogs' legs which I had promised him before I left.

I am a normal, restrained grandmother. My grandson's presence makes me cheerful, and his absence does not break my heart. I want him to be healthy and happy. Seeing him smile makes me cheerful, and it intrigues me to ponder "who" he might be inwardly now, and who he will be later on. His name is Alejandro because his godmother is my middle daughter, Alejandra, who, ever since she has been working at the UN in New York, treats us with an amiable condescension that irritates me. She believes she has performed an outstanding feat, as if all international organizations were not swarming with girls trained in efficient English-language colleges just as she was and similarly intoxicated with independence, with that process of elimination which involves country and family both at once, and with that arrogance—new in modern man—which makes exile a reward. The mere fact of living abroad now conjures up before our humbly provincial eyes the unmistakable beginnings of success. When I say that Alejandra is working at the United Nations in New York, my women friends say, "How marvelous, she was always so bright!" If she had founded in some one-horse town a school for children born deaf, dumb, and blind, whatever the progress of these youngsters or their reclamation for the benefit of society, no one would admire her. On the other hand, that vague and abstruse work with ramifications on five continents seems to endow her with an almost otherworldly capacity for ubiquitousness. I myself admire her from afar and envy her in secret.

If my parents had taught me everything I taught her, I would be translating the words of a black or Asian leader instead of tearing myself to pieces beneath the glaring sun of these beaches which a few kilometers away join Brazil. Dolores understands this fairly well, and when Iván begins making predictions about future devaluations of the peso and pontificating about the most effective way to eradicate hoof-and-mouth disease from our cattle, I think she too envies her sister a little and dreams of her solitude as if it were paradise. Both of us forget that Alejandra works eleven hours a day in her office, then two or three at home, cooking or opening cans (which is much harder than cooking, since our civilization has still failed to invent the perfect can opener), making her bed, washing dishes. Nickie has her feet planted much more firmly on the ground than Dolores or I. She belongs to the generation which knows everything, which allows itself everything and has a right to everything. She has no interest in acquiring duties, which leaves me dumfounded. At her age I was demanding to have the same duties as men, the duties taken on by Alejandra. In Nickie's opinion, while a woman may not be so pretentious and behind the times as to aspire to jewels, furs, or travelling in first class, a man is under an obligation to provide her with everything else. Her philosophy plunges me into deep perplexity. Is it possible she might be right? Although she may never have lifted a finger to earn her daily bread, can a woman be thought of as supported if she hitchhikes through Europe, sleeps in a tent, wears the same leather mini-skirt or the same faded blue jeans forever, and does not ask her husband to bathe, shave, or get a haircut?

We all know that two or three years from now Facundo will be clean and beardless and working in his father's factory, but he can never reproach Nickie for not having known how to be the perfect companion for camping trips and the days of youth. And when Facundo's position in society obliges her to be under the degrading sway of leopard or mink, she can go on asserting that it is to help Facundo's public relations.

Alejandro knocks on my door, and his sweet voice informs me: "Daddy and Mommy are ready. They want to know if we are going to eat soon." I'm coming, I'm coming. What are you writing, Grandma? A letter to your godmother. I'll send her a kiss from you. Is she really going to spend New Year's with us? I don't think so. Maybe she is coming in February. Let's go, Daddy and Mommy must be hungry, the trip has probably tired them out. No, Punta del Este is very close, and Daddy's car goes faster than anybody's. At this very moment all the children getting out of their daddies' cars are uttering that very phrase and, what's worse, all the daddies are uttering it too.

2 a.m.

At first everything went well. Our astonishment was reciprocal. They were astonished by the turkey I cooked for them. We cut the panettone, attempted to cut the nougat, and a hammer had to be found. Finally splinters of sugar and peanuts flew all over, and we gathered them up greedily. We passed around the nutcracker, and each of us popped the ends off a party cracker. Last of all we drank toasts. Then we undid the packages. Once stripped of the paper covered with sleds, stars, snowy trees, sack-laden Santas, and of the neatly tied red and green ribbons, each item began losing its enchanted quality—a bottle of perfume was merely a bottle of perfume, a silk handkerchief was just a silk handkerchief. It was only Alejo's toys which retained a certain magic. He carried them off to his room, spread them out around his bed as if they might protect him from gray everyday life, and no sooner had he put his head on the pillow than he was asleep. I kissed the blond hair which smelled of the sea, just as Santiago's and mine did when we would hold on to the boat with one arm and embrace with the other, our legs intertwined under the water. Flesh in its prime smells so different from flesh heading toward decay! Angrily, I smelled my shoulder, my arm, the back of my hand. I don't smell like an old woman yet, I thought. My grandson still presses up against me. Some day they will barely brush my forehead with their lips, and then I will know what I already have a presentiment of.

I had built a fire in the fireplace. Iván was moving it around needlessly with the poker, shortening the life of the logs. We were talking about Alejandra, Nickie, and Facundo.

"Alejandra had promised to spend Christmas with us. Then she said she would come for New Year's.... Do you think she'll be here?" Dolores asked in a critical tone.

"I don't know," I said in a low voice. "Maybe there's something keeping her there."

"What do you mean? That she has a boyfriend?"

Today is Christmas Eve, and I shouldn't get irritated. I swore not to get irritated no matter what they said, but I know Dolores wants to force me to say what we are all assuming: Alejandra has a lover. I'm not giving her the pleasure.

"Maybe. Why shouldn't she have a boyfriend? At her age, you were already married."

"I already had a child," Dolores pointed out.

"Naturally. So did I and almost all the women I know, most of my friends...."

"The times were different then," interrupted Dolores.

"No," I declared, "In some things the times do not change."

I feel that I won, that I changed the drift of the conversation; but the barb is always aimed right at me, even though it may come from a different direction.

"Obviously, they do change. When we were little, we used to go to midnight mass with you and grandmother. Why did you refuse to go today?"

"Alejo was dead tired...."

"We'll still be on time if we go ourselves," Iván interrupted slyly.

Dolores' reinforcements have arrived, I thought, and I must proceed with caution. In any case everyone is saying just the opposite of what he or she is thinking. Instead of playing the truth game, we play the lying game. I don't feel like shouting at them that this family Christmas Eve is a farce, that they have come from Punta del Este to keep their consciences clear and to be able to spy on me. Deep down they don't think I am alone. I don't know what they think and I don't care.... Yes, I do care. I would like to know what their comments will be when they go to bed tonight. I feel like screaming at them that it's not just young people who have the right to be rebellious, that there are rebellious old people too. What if I feel like being a rebellious mother, a rebellious grandmother, and not celebrating the dates which they take into their heads to decree Family Celebrations? But this is a useless waste of energy. I should save my energy for facing this long introspective summer vacation which I have laid out for myself: to think and to paint.

"It's five after twelve.... We will arrive in time," Dolores declares.

And someone who is not me replies what I had promised myself not to reply: "Go on if you feel like it. No one is stopping you. I'd rather go to bed or go to the midnight supper at Humberto the painter's."

They exchange a look. Their eyes, eloquent, are exclaiming: Humberto, the painter—so that's what it's all about! I feel like punching them. I confine myself to requesting in an impatient tone:

"Iván, please don't turn that whole log into ashes. If you leave it alone, it can last all night."

"It's just the opposite. Coals last much longer."

They know it all. Why argue?

"I don't understand why you don't want to go to mass," Dolores is insistent. "I realize you may not want to take communion.... That is, if you have some reason not to. But I've seen you cross yourself when a funeral goes by, and you have a Christ above your bed."

"I dislike collective manifestations.... I'm immune to the sacrifice of the mass. I don't feel it, at least not today."

My voice has stayed utterly calm. Is it that they want me to explain in just a few minutes all the contradictions at work in me? All my superstitions, my beliefs, my doubts, and my fervent piety for the cross? I look for another lame explanation.

"If you wanted to go to midnight mass, you should have told me sooner, and I wouldn't have worn pants.... You wouldn't have either, I imagine."

Dolores takes the blow. From the time she was a child, I have noticed her vulnerability in the face of inconsistent arguments and her stubborn persistence in the face of valid ones.

"Yes, of course, we should have thought of that earlier. I stayed in pants because I saw that's how you were dressed even though you've always told me you detest pants, that they don't suit you, that your legs are your best feature...."

"That's all still true," I said with a seraphic smile. "But here I'm more or less on a desert island. My best friends are the crabs, and my legs don't have any effect on them."

"At any rate, you've gotten tired of telling us that one must never let oneself go, not even in the country. You never allowed us to sit at the table in curlers even when we were alone."

Ouch! Now we are entering the dark corridors of filial reproach. They are long and full of twists and turns with unexpected ramifications. My daughters have implacable memories for recalling a day I went to a cocktail party although one of them had a fever, a night nobody prepared a meal since the cook had gone out and I forgot it was Thursday. "However, Rosa went out every Thursday. I don't know how you forgot." Undoubtedly it was the Thursday, precisely the Thursday I met you and I knew immediately I had never loved anyone nor could I love anyone the way I was going to love you.

By good fortune fate has always kept in reserve for me what

the French call *coups de théâtre*, that is, the unforeseen entrance on stage of unexpected characters. And on this Christmas Eve there occurred for the umpteenth time the miracle which should have brought down the first-act curtain. Just as in the theatre, with no previous warning, no prior sound of brakes nor slamming of a car door, without anyone having jolted the knocker or rung the bell, the door opened and a young man appeared, tanned, and in sky blue from top to toe—slacks and polo shirt—and I thought in all seriousness that he was my guardian angel.

"Freddy, what are you doing here?" Iván asked in surprise.

No, Freddy is not a usual name for a guardian angel, I sighed. He's simply a friend of Iván's. I was right. He had gone to Chouy, and his car had started making an unusual hum. It was a bearing.... He had to stay in La Paloma, he knew I was living here, he remembered that my darling children were planning to spend Christmas with me. The others had gone on to Punta del Este in Roberto's car.

"Are you sure it's a bearing and that it might not be the differential?"

Whatever the trouble was, I blessed it. I stood up, I offered him panettone, champagne....

"I think they'll have to go find the part in Montevideo or maybe Buenos Aires. Do you realize how ridiculous this is?"

"Maybe they can use this nougat made of sugarcoated steel," I dared to make a joke.

Dolores gave me a withering look. They had brought me the nougat.

Freddy laughed. "Who knows," he said. "I'm going to take it off to the mechanic."

Then Dolores and Iván laughed too. I used the opportunity to prepare a most dignified exit: "Well, now that a friend has arrived, I'm going to leave you young people to yourselves. I'm dead on my feet. I had an exhausting day."

"No, please, don't leave," said Freddy. "For so many years I've wanted to meet you, ever since I read your first book."

"Which one?" I asked, accustomed to each reader supposing that the first one coming to his notice was my first work.

"*The Psychology of Artists and Madmen.* I bought it because of the title. Where did you get the idea? It's so clever."

"I was influenced by the life and work of Van Gogh. I'll be writing a study of him this winter."

"You know, artists don't always use their imaginations," Iván commented. "Sometimes while they're chewing on the end of a pen or looking at the wall, their mind a blank, they do the same as any bad student: they fall under the influence of a reproduction or the shape taken on by a spot of moisture."

The reflection seemed an apt one, and I thought that a woman with sons-in-law instead of daughters-in-laws has no right to complain. If Iván had been my son and Dolores my daughter-in-law the circle of comments surrounding me would be a hundred times more malevolent. But I stuck to my attitude of the elderly lady who retires in order to let the young people enjoy themselves more freely.

"I'm glad to meet you too, but we will have a chance for a longer talk."

"Of course, I have to stay here at least three or four days. It's probably like being buried alive, isn't it? Especially if it rains."

"You'll soon see for yourself," I said with a smile.

"But you're not going to stay," shrieked Dolores. "That would be crazy. Come with us to Punta and we'll bring you back later to pick up your car."

"But, of course," Iván backed her up. "That makes the most sense."

"No, look, they understand very little about cars here, since they don't make them.... I don't want to leave it to chance. I understand something about mechanical work and I'd rather be present. Besides, a sports car is always more of a fucking nuisance to repair."

He had said an offensive word in such a natural way that he didn't shock any of us. I excused myself, conscious that Dolores and Iván would spend the rest of the night trying to convince him not to stay. What are they afraid of? Do they have reason to be afraid of it? I never did like young men, but they say that's the best medicine for an aging woman.... The truth is, I'm dead on my feet. I suppose I should put: "To be continued in the next issue." If I were indeed to continue my stay in La Paloma, the diary I am trying to keep would turn into a magazine serial. And what's the difference, if the serial makes me happy? I doubt it will. Serials never gave me the slightest pleasure. I hear doors open and close, water running, Iván's and Freddy's voices outside the house, the screen door shutting, the faucet being turned on again. Ah, how I now miss my solitude, which weighed on me so heavily.

December 26

I got up early yesterday; the others were still sleeping. I woke Alejandro (who sleeps on a sofa in my room). I thought at last I could be alone with him for a while. Right away he wanted to go to the beach, and he told me he would be a sailor when he grew up, like his grandfather. I thought of Santiago, dead in a shipwreck just as if we were living in the eighteenth or nineteenth century or even earlier. Dead in a shipwreck in the twentieth century! I could never get over such an anomaly befalling our household. When he died, we were no longer that happy, of course. The honeymoon had been left behind. Far, far back in time were the salty embraces which, I was embarrassed to learn afterwards, had been watched avidly from the deck of the frigate Sarmiento by some of Santiago's fellow naval cadets, snatching the binoculars from each other. Dolores was fifteen and—as is natural—in love with her often-absent father. Alejandra was eleven, Nickie seven. My relationship with Juan Manuel had been plodding along nicely. For four years Santiago had been involved with Juan Manuel's wife. All this ended up the worst possible arrangement. Eleonora (for that was her name), having realized she was alone, tried to get her husband back in her grip, something which couldn't have been very hard to carry off. Ordinarily, the man who puts up with being a married woman's lover can't handle continuing the relationship when the woman is left free. The situation changes, and responsibilities increase. The woman becomes a nuisance. She finds her solitary nights oppressive and wants the lover to play the husband, to take her to a movie or a restaurant. One has to turn everything around and go back to the starting point, but in love there's no going back to the starting point. It's something of a feat just to progress quickly and smoothly from one stage to the next. Juan Manuel chose Eleonora "for the sake of the children, you understand." Children are tougher than we realize, of course; besides, whether I understood or had given up on understanding was all the same to him—he had made up his mind. So, a month after being left a widow, I broke off with Juan Manuel. My only distractions were the paperwork for the pension and Nickie's hugs and kisses. Dolores judged me mercilessly. My mourning clothes seemed to her too frivolous for the widow of a hero; she had garbed herself in black from head to toe: shoes, stockings, dress, handbag, gloves, no necklace, just a silver watch with a black leather band. I didn't change the color of my stockings nor did I give up my pearl necklace. When home alone I would put on a dress of any old color, and at night I would choose at random a blue nightgown or a pink one. She wore white nightgowns. She was the real widow,and I was not competing with her for the honor. It has to be said in her defense that any girl of fifteen would have adopted the same silly, romantic, uncompromising posture. I understood her, but she never did forgive me for having understood her. She mistook my comprehension for scorn or indifference. She may even have thought it a trick. Relations between parents and children become so twisted when one parent is gone that it is not humanly possible to straighten them out. If they are difficult in a united household.... Alejandra and Nickie went on living normally without paying much attention to their older sister's boundless grief. Dolores was outraged when they did not want to accompany her to the cemetery every Tuesday (since their father had died on a Tuesday). She no longer aimed so high and was happy if they accompanied her once a month on the sixth (the date of the accident, of course). After three months, the girls refused to go with her, and I myself put my foot down. I forbade her to make her sisters' childhood miserable, since there was nothing we could do about the irreparable.

I missed Santiago much more than Dolores imagined. We had adored each other. Later on we were open and understood each other. Never were we deceitful. People stop loving each other or at least desiring each other, and the flesh sometimes has other needs. We considered separating, but two very good reasons kept us together: on the one hand, the girls; on the other, Santiago's career, which kept him from remarrying in another country (the only recourse for unhappily married Argentineans, thanks to our laws). Whenever we had this out, in the end he would say with a rather melancholy smile: "I'm sorry, my dear. Everything could be arranged if you had married a nightclub singer or a movie star. What they call marriage, I call cohabitation. So there's nothing to do but keep it secret." All this happened in the last five years of his life. Up to then we had been truly happy. I missed his friendship, his fleeting appearances, the braid-trimmed uniforms hanging in his wonderfully tidy, sweet-smelling closet. I needed his support, his common sense. I did not know how to manage. His pension was adequate, but there was nothing left over because living expenses were high and the girls were at difficult ages. And so I made use of my talent for drawing and started doing portraits of well-known people. I spent my lonely nights writing the book on ill-fated painters, which became a success, was made into a play, then a film, under the title, *Men of Inspiration*. Gauguin, Van Gogh, and Modigliani were the pillars on which I supported my theory.

There were no messages at the hotel. They told me we shouldn't miss the film that night. They were showing *Ninotchka* with Greta Garbo, the receptionist pointed out excitedly, as though it were the latest film of the world's greatest actress. I offered my endorsement: "It's quite good even though it is rather old." She gave me a surprised look.

It was around noon when we all went to the beach in a happy

group. Iván helped me by taking charge of the beach umbrella although he set it up wrong and the wind blew it away. He set it up again, and the wind blew it away again. I tried to explain to him the only infallible system that would keep it from taking off even in a gale: first, round and round, then crosswise, then round and round again. He assumed that was the crazy notion of a mother-in-law in the early stages of arteriosclerosis. He very nearly asked whether I'd had a blood test to measure my cholesterol level. But the fourth time the umbrella took off, I stepped in and used my infallible system: round and round, then crosswise five or six times, then round and round. It didn't take off again. Iván said it was an old umbrella, improperly designed for standing up to the wind; theirs is not so complicated. He was trying to suggest that my umbrella had developed eccentricities, just like an old person's dog. Next came the matter of Alejo's water torture. The inevitable scenario: a man doesn't get cold, a man isn't scared of waves and, to be a man, you have to learn to swim. Why, Iván's father had tossed *him* off a boat into the sea, and Iván had learned to swim. (And that's how others learn to drown.) His father had of course dived in the water after him and showed him how etc... etc.... But that morning Alejo was without enthusiasm, no doubt because of an upset stomach from the champagne, nougat, and nuts which were assaulting his insides. Whether he feels like it or not, he must take a dip to show he is a man. How strange: to prove their manhood, male children are supposed to do the things they don't wish to. Once of age, to demonstrate their masculinity they are supposed to do just the opposite: that is, do only what they feel like doing, whether or not it pleases anyone else. My housewifely knowledge of basic psychoanalysis tends to make me think this accelerated course in *machismo*—which fathers are compelled to provide for boys in those tender years when their sexual characteristics are as yet undeveloped—leads to the monstrous egotism of later life. I think of how I did the same with my daughters, how I disapproved of Dolores' exaggerated mourning, and how I often endeavored to turn aside natural tendencies in the three of them on the pretext of making them tough. Nature is not as wise as she claims. At an age when our own inner being has scarcely taken shape, we are entrusted with shaping other human beings who are as soft as butter left out in the sun. I admit that I was able to exert no influence on my daughters and that for several years I was wrong about the personality of each one. Dolores seemed rebellious; but it was only her yearning for inflexible order, a household where the father was not always absent and where no adultery merited the Almighty's reprimanding those who cast stones. Nickie and Alejandra, who hugged and kissed me, squeezed up against me, slid in between my sheets—about the only thing they didn't do was lick me like kittens—were instinctively seeking the protection needed to turn their weakness into strength so they could launch out resolutely on their chosen paths without wondering if they were hurting me.

Children cannot take on their own personalities without clawing their parents along the way. I clawed mine and, like my daughters, I often did so with malice aforethought. The generations do not change as much as is claimed. If we take a closer look, I think parents have evolved farther than children. When I look back to my grandmother, my parents, and on ahead to my cousins, and even myself, I realize we all counted on our parents' total, unfailing availability. To us, the earth would seem to have fallen off its axis if we had arrived for a visit with our grandmother only to find her not at home, or if she had not gathered us under her roof at the ranch in summertime. As long as Mama lived (and she did die young, she hadn't reached the age I am now), it seemed natural to find her there when I'd knock on the door or to call and let her know I was coming for breakfast or dinner. Like the Lares and Penates, it was my parents' duty to guard the hearth. I have been bitterly reproached by my daughters for starting to travel again, for being gone at the wrong time, for spending weekends in the country with friends—in short, for my lack of availability. According to children, that is what a mother should be: someone who is available. They regard us as committing criminal offenses if we plan our diversions and summer vacations without keeping them in mind. I think my coming to La Paloma shocked Dolores and Iván. In Punta del Este I could have helped them out by going to the beach at La Mansa with Alejo while they went off to La Terraza or La Brava. Here I'm an old lady acting perverse.

It was more than half past twelve today when I exclaimed, "We have to see about Alejo's lunch!" They gave me surprised looks. "It's still early." "But this way he can take a little nap and come back to the beach with us later." A moment of silence, then an outburst from Dolores: "These things must have been so simple in your day when there were nannies and cooks, but nowadays children eat at the same time as their parents, so don't worry about it; nothing bad happens to them."

In the distance Iván's big car shone in the sun. At my feet lay Dolores' Pucci blouse, her expensive summer shoes, and Iván's French T-shirt. In my day there were nannies, but we drove around in shabby, banged-up little cars, with the upholstery split open, and the tires as smooth as a baby's skin. I dare to say this, but Dolores and Iván both speak at once: "That shows a lack of business sense.... A car appreciates in value...so we're making an investment.... At least our children aren't being raised by paid help.... All the theories on education confirm this...."

I wonder why I answered back. How can I have forgotten that they're always right? For them, the Ten Commandments begin, "Only by incurring debts shalt thou become rich." And they make fun of our daily account keeping and our impeccable but modest statements of interest earned.

To cut the discussion short, I run down to the water. I want to drag Alejo with me, but he has ended up so traumatized (a word parents use when talking about themselves, but never in reference to their own children) that he doesn't want to go near the shore.

I offer an opinion: "We should go to the little beach at Bahía, and not to Solari. It's a better place for Alejo."

They don't answer back. When I come out of the ocean I find them engaged in lively conversation. Seeing me approach, they grow silent. Alejo is building a sand castle with another little boy, who is bringing him a pail of water. Building the battlements makes one of the towers collapse, and Alejo loses his temper.

I stretch out in the sun, thinking that tomorrow I'll be alone again and I'll feel the world around me swaying, but I prefer that to this systematic familial exasperation.

Iván suddenly says, "I feel like getting something to drink."

"Good idea," I reply. "Let's go to Luigi's café. It's that little house over there with the thatched roof. It's very pleasant, and they have clams and mussels. We can even eat lunch."

We start to gather up our things. At half past one, the afternoon sun is beating down. It's very hot, and we are all hungry and thirsty. Iván is in charge of taking the umbrella and mattresses to the car. Dolores, Alejo, and I walk along slowly. Our raffia bags are heavy on our arms, as if they were filled with lead. Alejo drops his sand toys and shovel, he goes back to pick them up, Dolores scolds him. The little shelter where cool drinks await rises up before us like a mirage in the desert.

"I don't know how you can stand this climate," Dolores remarks.

We go under the thatched overhang and are inside. Nino hurries up, his hair wet. Obviously, he has just come out of the water. I introduce him, and he finds us a table in the shadows. We are tired of brightness. We order clams and chilled white wine. As usual, Alejo wants a Pepsi. Iván arrives, sweating and wiping his forehead with a handkerchief.

He says, "I don't know how you can stand this climate."

"In the summer it's hot everywhere, " I say, taking pride in my originality.

Luigi comes over to greet us. Nino waits on us pleasantly, but I notice he's more proper than usual. I think seeing me play the grandmother bothers him.

"Is there a good place around here for lunch?" Iván asks while eating his clams and mussels.

"May I suggest that a full lunch after this and with the heat would be too much. We could go home and eat the leftover turkey from last night."

"Aha! Here you are. I looked everywhere," exclaims a cheerful voice, belonging to Freddy. He is tan, and naked except for a dreadful pair of old-gold swim trunks adorned with date palms and coconut trees which are dropping their ripe fruit on his belly and on what little of his anatomy is covered.

Suddenly the world looks better; differentials, connecting rods, and pistons sound like music to my ears. Alejo says nothing ever breaks in Daddy's car, and they pass everyone else on the road. Freddy pats him on the head and goes on recounting his unfortunate experiences as if telling us he had won the lottery.

Nino approaches. I introduce him to Freddy: I say simply, "A friend."

I feel my actions have some significance in Nino's presence. And to keep Iván from making it obvious that Freddy is *his* friend, I become garrulous. I explain how Freddy had a part break on the way back to Chouy, that if he stays here a few days he'll be a good customer. I ask Nino for an extra glass, and I ask him which mechanic is best. My idea to eat at home meets with everyone's approval. The heat is stifling, and besides, Iván doesn't feel like spending his money. He'd rather keep it for Punta del Este. Here he doesn't show off.

We were having our coffee when a neighbor's little boy arrived on his bicycle. At the hotel they had entrusted him with two letters which had come on the ONDA bus. One was from New York, the other from Paris. Alejandra and Nickie of course. How could they not write me at Christmas?

I leave the letters on the table, planning to read them later when I'm by myself.

"You're not going to open them?" Dolores asks, scarcely restraining her indignation.

"I'd rather read them when I'm by myself. I'll show them to you after we nap."

"I don't understand you," she says reproachfully. "You get two letters from your daughters, and you put them aside as if they were bills." Unperturbed, I insist, "I'd like to read them when I'm by myself."

Freddy is saying goodbye. The mechanic promised to try putting together a replacement part to get him as far as Punta del Este. I think he has noticed the family tensions. Before he leaves, I hear him asking Iván, "And you're going to be staying around here for a while?"

"Are you crazy?" Iván answers. "We're going this afternoon. We came to spend Christmas with my mother-in-law, that's to be expected. Dolores is the only daughter who's here. We couldn't let her be alone."

Iván returns to the living room. Alejo is annoyed because I want him to take a nap. He never has and doesn't see any reason to do so now. But Dolores and Iván are tired and back me up. This village lost between vast beaches, with its heavy tropical air, its overly bright sun, and its white, white sand, has worn them out. They want to rest and be fresh for their arrival in Punta, where they are having a dinner party.

Somewhat apprehensively I pick up the two letters. Getting news from my daughters always alarms me. Generally their letters are filled with complicated commissions which I am totally incapable of carrying out. They complain a little so I won't complain, but they don't usually put in the least hint of familiarity. They don't go beyond the customary polite phrases, the time-honored "I miss you a lot, and I really miss Argentina. A big hug from your loving daughter," followed in Nickie's case by a p.s., "Facundo sends his love."

I have spent twenty-four hours tiptoeing on ground glass.

I don't have any strength left. After napping I'll open my mail. Now I must sleep a while.

December 27

As a child I heard stories—made up, no doubt—about people who thought they could stop the march of time by crawling into bed. In a certain sense, I've done the same thing, but I chose for my sleeping place a tiny village in the middle of a vast profusion of nature. It doesn't matter that for me time seems to have stood still the last two weeks; what does matter is that for my daughters it continued to march on. The letters were more than simple Christmas greetings. Alejandra—who even a few weeks ago thought she held heaven in her hands—was complaining of overwork, of the possibility of quitting and finding something less hectic, more feminine. She explained, "Here you have to be a man or turn into a lesbian. I leave home when it's barely getting light, and I come back when it's already dark. I arrive here so tired I just want to crawl into bed. I don't even have what it takes to see a television serial to the end. I can't keep my eyes open. I have to use my Saturdays and Sundays for washing my hair, doing my nails, and sewing on buttons. I work longer hours than a medieval serf." Other complaints followed: the intense cold, the monotonous, repetitive life, these meaningless international organizations which solve nothing and cannot even halt the war in Vietnam. And, in passing, a name: Bob, whom she dates once in a while but is not the answer to her solitary Saturdays and Sundays, because he is married and can't leave himself open to what people might say. Of course he doesn't get along with his wife, who doesn't understand him, is frigid, is a much better mother than wife...in short, the age-old song. "I did understand, Alejandra!" I shout from this side of the ocean, grasping the letter lovingly. She says and repeats the same word which is torturing me: solitude. How hard it is to learn to be alone! And today, once again, I feel alone. I wonder why Iván, Dolores, and Alejandro came? I wonder why we performed this little one-act play—a drama of misunderstandings and gaping holes not easily filled in so short a time—ending with the mental "phew!" we all uttered upon parting. Why all that unless to make me realize their presence does not fill up my life and their departure leaves it emptier than before? As I stood here on the stone threshold, Alejo's little hand waving from the rear window made me feel very much alone.

Ah, how I would love to be strong! If a fairy offered to grant me three wishes, I would ask only to know how to live within my solitude as easily as I know how to live among people—to know how to be alone without seeing worry and distress sneak up, without inventing fictitious obligations, without running in a frenzy to a crowded place although I may seem to be walking there slowly; to learn how not to sense that request for help lying dormant in me, always ready to burst out of my heart and flow into my mouth.

My poor Alejandra! With the same silly naïveté as everyone else, I thought living in a great foreign capital, having an enviable job and long working hours would be enough to keep one from feeling alone. I envied you. I would like to have been born in your generation. I thought it was almost like being born a man and that instead of going up and down these sun-roasted streets in search of greens, mussels, bread, and cheese, I would be holding the post expected in accordance with my training, my age, my reputation. But your frustration disorients me. You are going through what I am. You haven't managed to become a man, my poor Alejandra. You're spending your Saturdays and Sundays eating away at yourself, thinking that Bob is with his wife. Deep down you don't believe in her supposed frigidity nor in the age-old phrases: "For a long time there's been nothing between us. I love her like a sister, but I couldn't hurt her. I can't harm anyone," not noticing that at that very moment he's tearing you apart.

When Dolores read Alejandra's letter, it was too much for her: "There isn't anything that suits her. In Buenos Aires she'd say terrible things about Argentina, that it was impossible to live there, that she wanted to work. She got what she wanted, and after two years she can't take it any more. And, besides, if I were her mother, I'd tell her she shouldn't date married men."

"Yes, but you are not her mother...I am, and I know what I ought to say."

"If you'll allow me to confess I read her letter, I'll write to her...."

Of course she herself always writes for the entire family and usually puts as a heading, "My dear holy family," or some other little joke which excuses her from writing us one by one.

"Tell her whatever you want," I replied, and we read Nickie's letter. She is two months pregnant. We gather that at first she would remember to take her pills and that, besides, love was not so joyful in their tent, in the sleeping bags they would crawl into exhausted at the end of long days of hiking and campfires that didn't want to burn and indignation at seeing how motorists would rather choose their own companions than pick up those calling to them from the curb. When the cold weather came, and Facundo's father footed the bill for good hotels on condition his son visit factories in Munich and the Arts Ménagers Show in Paris (parents are tyrants), they checked into a comfortable hotel. Good food, fine wine, a warm room, smooth sheets, bath salts to tint and perfume the hot water—all that made it possible for her to forget her pills and, along with them, her resolutions.

Now she is suffering from nausea, and they plan to return by ship. They think they'll sail at the end of January. They'll arrive in time to spend a few days with me in La Paloma. I shudder. Will I still be here in the middle of February, at the beginning of March? Can I hold out? Dolores and Iván were discussing the good news: Nickie was setting out on the path of normality. She would not be among that multitude of women who are alone and on the wrong track. Their words were aimed directly at a target—me—and they were forgetting that their target had been married and had produced three charming daughters, which didn't keep her from being as alone as a mollusk today, at forty-nine.

I don't feel close to Nickie, and that is natural. Her current problem is too far removed from mine, or to be more precise, she doesn't have any problems. Alejandra worries me. I know her. I am afraid she may give up at the wrong time and be sorry later. I changed into a flowered red blouse along with freshly ironed pants—white—despite the nuisance of having to take them to the laundry tomorrow, and I set out for Humberto's, where last night's celebration was continuing. They were getting my car started when

I heard them call me, and I suddenly saw Freddy, as cheerful and enthusiastic as usual.

"Still here?" I asked as the solitude surrounding me gradually dissipated like a bank of fog.

"Of course. They can't even order the part until tomorrow, so you're going to have to put up with me for a while."

"But why didn't you take Iván up on his offer? Leaving with them would have been the natural thing to do, rather than staying in this desolate spot. You could have come later for your car."

"And why are *you* staying?"

"Personal reasons."

"Maybe I have mine too."

"It's not the same. As the French would say, *J'ai assez tourné autour des petits fours*. I've already gone to an incalculable number of cocktail parties and dinners. I want to learn solitude, approach it very slowly, and tame it before it pounces on me and devours me."

"Why do you need to be alone? A woman like you can be with people day and night if she so desires...."

"Up to a certain age limit...after that...well, it would take too long to explain. Get in the car, and I'll take you to a spot that's really in: a painter who's a tavern keeper, bohemians, red wine and salami."

"The usual," said Freddy, laughing and getting into the car. "The bohemians make fun of the bourgeoisie, but they have even less imagination than we do."

"I don't belong to the bourgeoisie."

"Well, *I* do. That is, in the sense in which the bohemians use the word. I indulge in all the pleasures I can, and I work at it. In London I buy myself cashmere sweaters and cloth for my suits; in Paris I select my ties and go dine at the homes of people who use noble titles, where they feed me well and pass me the platters; I frequent embassies...."

"I did the same. That's why I'm telling you to go back to Punta. Look, I'm even tempted *not* to take you to Humberto's.

Everything's going to seem dirty to you, a little sordid, and dark, and you'll be right too, because it is all those things. A poor imitation of international bohemia."

I had stopped the car a hundred meters from the tavern, whose colored lights shone through the trees.

"Do you know why these things strike me as funny?" Freddy asked. "Because in Paris or London it's not a game. An artist's poverty is real. What's more, outlandish actions mean something over there even when they're exaggerated. Those fellows perform them to attract attention. Success is hard to come by, but...." He shrugged his shoulders.

"Right, here success is easy and isn't good for much. On the contrary, it falls on one like a coffee stain on a white outfit, just enough to attract attention and so periodicals can make use of us in mocking tones when they're short of subject matter."

And all of a sudden, the inevitable scenario: Freddy took me in his arms. I could feel him against me, strong, healthy, young, warm. His mouth searched for mine. For a moment or two I succumbed to these caresses. I didn't desire him, but I was grateful for his urgent, youthful desire. I'm already at the age when a woman is grateful for being desired, I thought nostalgically. And then I pushed him away gently.

"No," I said, "Come on. There are some young things at the tavern. Let's go."

"I don't like young things. They're all the same: silly."

"Don't utter clichés. Women turn even sillier when they get old. They repeat the same story five or six times the same night, when they've already told it the week before and it's not of the slightest interest anyway."

He kept insisting. His fingers were undoing the buttons on my blouse. I was annoyed to think about how I would arrive all wrinkled and that maybe tomorrow María wouldn't come and that my closet was full of un-ironed pants and blouses. No, no, I didn't desire him in spite of his beauty, in spite of the tribute his desire signified.

"No, please, Freddy, this is ridiculous."

But he kept insisting; he wasn't listening to me; he was so sure that I was supposed to surrender in a daze, perhaps fall on my knees before the miracle. He was mistaken. He was no longer Freddy, I couldn't even see him in the darkness. He was one of the many who had thought it my duty as a modern woman to repay them like this for a dinner, a play, a night they had deigned to devote to me. To be wrestling again like a thirty-year-old seemed the height of ridiculousness; besides, I was not to blame. The habit of making love—like those of smoking, drinking, gambling, and travelling—is lost little by little almost without our knowing why, no doubt because maturity has sneaked up on us. Our tastes change, our critical sense grows stronger, an uncontrollable laziness overcomes us. Yes, it's true. I have yet to know Honolulu and India, but what a superhuman effort I shall have to make to force myself to know them! And for what? In any case I'd rather coerce myself into knowing Nepal than into yielding to Freddy's raging vanity. I picture him one day, after he has had one too many, relating this adventure in distorted form. Maybe it will even reach Iván in an unpleasant version that his mother-in-law "is a loony old girl who lures boys into cars." I push him away forcefully.

"Please, that's enough playing."

"I'm not playing."

"I'm not either. Come along, if you want to go to The Magic Seashell; if not, walk back to the hotel."

He understands that I mean it. He moves away. There's a shaky, almost infantile smile on his lips.

"Forgive me. I lost control, you're very attractive."

"Of course. I get offers from Hollywood every day."

I shrug my shoulders and start the car. Meekly, Freddy asks: "I want to spend the evening with you. I don't like being alone, much less in a hotel room. Take me to The Magic Seashell. I promise to behave properly."

For a few moments we drove along in silence. You stupid little jerk, I thought. A kind of sentimental friendship, a romantic flirtation, whatever, would have been so nice. Anything except this encore of wrestling and made-to-order *machismo*, for no reason except that he is on his own, seated next to a woman in a car at night. But, Freddy, what you don't know is that I came determined to say, "Enough!" Or do you think I chose La Paloma by chance, that out of sheer absentmindedness I went by Punta del Este and ended up here?

Enough, enough, enough, I kept repeating while I turned off the ignition, extinguished the headlights, and stepped out of the car in front of Humberto's. When one says, "Enough!" one should carry through. These are things not to be put off until tomorrow. I suffered too much for believing that love was eternal.

We made our way through the heavy smoke and huddled in a corner so we wouldn't disturb Manolo, who was singing and playing the guitar. Humberto waved to me from across the room and sent Perico with two glasses of wine. Freddy squeezed my hand. "Do you forgive me?" he asked.

"It was so obvious," I said, shrugging my shoulders.

Someone on our right shushed us. We stopped talking. Manolo sang without pause, intoxicated by his own voice, and by the songs repeated a hundred, a thousand times, which always seemed new to him and always brought the same pleasure to him and to the crowd. Some were joining in on the best-known tangos. The people gathered there seemed to have been copied with indelible carbon paper, and I thought of God's immense boredom in the presence of man's renewed histrionics.

December 28

Last night I really wasn't up to writing about the end of the party. It was quite late. I spent a solitary day, deafeningly solitary. At first, for the pleasure of it. I was enjoying my independence, and I put my house in order. María came, and I gave her all the washing and ironing. I headed for the beach because I never stay home when a maid is tidying up my house. It fills me with guilt complexes. I can't stand seeing other people work for me. Sometimes I don't go to the hairdresser out of embarrassment that some other woman has to wash my hair. It's not as if I were paralyzed! The Merry Mussel was empty. Nino had gone to Montevideo and Luigi to Punta because they had to fetch supplies. The younger son, age fourteen, served me mussels with spaghetti. I ate voraciously, without anyone reminding me that pasta is fattening. I felt split in two. One half of me found itself at ease, almost happy, sure of fulfilling the patient destiny for which it had come to these parts; my other half was beginning to worry, to mutter that the day would be long, that this season in La Paloma would turn out to be unbearable.

Of course it is at moments like these I regret swearing to myself I wouldn't paint any more, that I would confine myself to art criticism. I have no creative talent. I came to that conclusion after lengthy reflection. My daughters no longer needed me to work to provide them with life's little amenities and I, who (as anyone might) had momentarily been made giddy by the favorable reception of my first show, the great success (very nearly glory) of the second, and who had fallen into a terrible depression in face of the unexpected attacks levelled at the third, sat down one day with all the clippings to analyze what was taking place. The early ones hailed my successful entry into the world of plastic arts. Naturally my success alarmed no one and didn't eclipse anyone else's work. "It was a promise—why call it a promise? Indeed, it's already fulfilled," declared the same weekly which four years later sent me back to the kitchen because of "my inability to conform to the most elementary laws of divine proportion." All the clippings taken together made me laugh, and they still amuse me, but in their time they had been terribly mortifying. Later I came to understand it was neither art nor my work that was at issue, but my supposedly privileged position in life. Moreover, when a revolution occurred which brought naval officers to the fore, the late Santiago's name in a position of honor helped me greatly. Later it seems the navy and the air force opposed the government in power and the periodicals backing it tore me to pieces. Everything but my work influenced my critics: my family name, Santiago's glorious death, the navy, the army, political parties, Dolores' brilliant marriage to a member of the cattle oligarchy, Alejandra's job at the United Nations (which led people to assume we opposed the regime in Cuba), Nickie's marriage to the son of an industrialist, my long stays at beach resorts, my trips to Europe, my imported soaps, my attraction to perfumes and furs. All this was more than enough for my work to remain completely in the background, while I found myself in the glare of dreadful neon lights, my features distorted, my eyes swollen, the very image of the drug addict, the drunk, the woman gone mad, the caricature which can drive away any admirers. All this most meticulously prepared in laboratories while people who saw me at shows, as I really was, would say, "It isn't possible, you look like the daughter of the woman I saw in the picture.... You're just not photogenic." I have the same photograph touched up by a woman photographer who tried to make me look pretty and another copy by a male photographer who was shooting to kill. We look neither like grandmother nor granddaughter. Thus, in spite of being very slow about catching on to some things, I ended up becoming aware of the reality, and I swore I'd say, "Enough!" and not have any more shows during my lifetime, hoping that after my death (especially if it appeared to be a suicide) they'd use me and cook me up in whatever sauces they pleased. In general we dead artists serve to demonstrate that living artists are worms by comparison. That is why I sat opposite myself (no need for a mirror) one evening and gave some motherly advice. Why get involved in having shows if I could paint for enjoyment and write about other painters? Why choose such a hostile world when within reach there was another world—well-bred, magnanimous, genial—made up of elegant meals, men carefully shaved and smelling of scent, people who declared I could be my daughters' sister (younger sister, of course) and who spoke enthusiastically... about poems I never wrote, still lifes painted by colleagues, pictures truly mine but loathsome? At that point, things became very clear. I would almost venture to say I could hear voices, like Joan of Arc. At least I pictured myself being burned at the stake.

I knew if the day of the Grand Inquisition were to come, those who had disparaged, slandered and reviled me would be there with me, all of us burning at the stake together. I knew that those young people with wild dreams of becoming Leonardo or Cézanne would not excuse my mediocrity, since they could not forgive themselves for their own. That is why, on the day of the Last Judgment, they would all be herded together into the same pen. And I knew that the adorable people would go on their way having absolutely no understanding of what was happening to me, while the irascible, incorruptible artists already knew, and would come to realize more and more, that my agony was exactly like theirs. They hated me the way siblings hate each other—like Cain and Abel; the others liked me the way one likes something belonging to another species: a hothouse plant, a dog, an art object, a piece of fine china, a race horse. I knew (because that day I learned many things which are now once more half forgotten) that neither the praise nor the criticism was wholly sincere; in addition, both were aimed at a number of vested interests. Maybe those well-bred men and women didn't really feel the slightest esteem for me or my art. They said I had brought my daughters up badly, that I was five or ten pounds too heavy, that I wore clothes which had apparently been selected by my enemies, that I became pedantic when art was discussed, that Santiago had put up with me because he was a saint and also because he didn't want to lose out on promotions; in short, to themselves or in private, they would express harsh criticism of me and the way I led my life. On the other hand, that malicious newspaper writer who didn't stand a chance of earning his bread by being nice knew only too well how many hours, how many sleepless nights, how many broken nails, how much throbbing of the temples, how much discouragement went into those canvases or into the pages of that study; and apparently he brushed this knowledge aside, although it kept pursuing him in his down moments as if his conscious unfairness were going to visit unavoidable punishment upon him. Yes, although we both might bemoan it, we were condemned to burn at the stake together. Both of us would be sorry for everything because both of us lived in an insomniac universe where we were aware of our acts.

I do not like delving so deeply into myself or into my fellow beings. I like faintly sketched outlines which say little and suggest much. All this delving reminds me of literature from the last century and smacks of psychoanalysis. We all know that to seek the fourth dimension is to aspire to the impossible. Why then do we do it when it's a matter of our souls? I wouldn't want to be a sculptor. I don't need the third dimension. The first and second are enough for me, with lines to confine the universe, and planes to express it. Perhaps here on this vast and half-deserted beach, I shall manage to do without the inspiration provided by human life; perhaps at the same time I shall learn to do without the inconsolable ill-fated geniuses from newspaper offices and without society flattery, becoming equally indifferent to forced, puerile sarcasm and pleasant phrases dictated by elegant breeding. But no, I'm lying to myself. There is in me that pressing need to feel something throbbing with life even if it's only the tiny crab scurrying among the rocks I'm displacing...life...if I could at least manage to have an inkling of the significance of that energy wasted uselessly by a Nature generally phlegmatic except when a volcano erupts or an earthquake shakes the earth or a tidal wave shakes the ocean. Everything else is born, grows, and dies systematically governed by an unchanging order and is dependent on the seasons, on water, sun, and air. On a calm morning when no breeze is stirring, a flowering plant does not abruptly lose its leaves *just because*. But however much I might argue and protest, I'm not going to turn into a sunflower, a poplar, or an ear of wheat.

I'm going to rouse myself, and I'm going to make lentil soup. Since the pancetta's gone, there's a good excuse to go out shopping. I want to see people, to exchange a remark or two, to hear someone's voice. I want to stay home and find out if Freddy is coming to take me to dinner as he promised last night. How complicated life is for a person on her own. She spends it arguing with herself, giving herself advice she doesn't take, making decisions she doesn't carry out. She is at the mercy of the first arrival who sees a light in her window. When she is hesitating between two suggestions or two objects, she never has the excuse that she is going to consult with her partner; moreover, we have to flail about like a fish in a net whenever a male friend decides we are the ideal dinner partner, the dreamed-of companion for a festive evening. There's never any reason to say no; there's never any reason to say yes. I lack the willpower to say no; I lack the desire to say yes.

December 29

It was good I stayed home. When I went to fix myself two fried eggs instead of lentil soup (besides no pancetta for it, there were no lentils), I saw Freddy's sports car drive up. My heart skipped a beat. This boy was actually interested in me. He was chasing me all over La Paloma from Solari to La Aguada. While he was knocking, I touched up my lipstick and hair and quickly changed my blouse. The blue one is more flattering. When I opened the door and saw the happy look on his face, I was filled with tenderness. I felt indispensable. Once again, my presence was lighting up someone's life.

Freddy took me by the shoulders, gave me a big kiss, and said, "It's done. Finally I can leave this hole I've been buried in for the last six days. I'm going to Punta. Can I take you?"

"No, thanks," I stammered.

"That's a mistake. You'll die of boredom here. Anyway, if you have something for Dolores and Iván.... I can take them a letter."

"Ah, yes, Alejo left a T-shirt here." I went to get it. I felt the color had drained from my face. I tried to compose myself before going back to the living room. What did I expect from this boy whom I had been wise enough to reject during his stay here? Nothing, or something quite simple: to have dinner with him tonight and talk of some past great love and relive it in his eyes. Calmer already, I came back with the T-shirt. He was insistent about taking me to Punta. He jotted down his "address" on a scrap of paper, one of those vague Punta del Este addresses, which you find through pure instinct, just like those in Tokyo—streets without names and summer cottages with no numbers, which you must get to through trial and error. But you always get there if you really want to. "It's a just a little country place I rented with a friend. The good thing is that it's near the golf course, since I have a nutty fiancée who spends all her time playing golf...." He was finally confessing, with an embarrassed little laugh.

"Why didn't she come and look you up here?"

"Wanda here? No way. She's never taken a bus. She'd die first, and the old girl's not going to lend her the car for that long. She needs it so she can go to the cocktail parties. She goes to all of them." Now the family biography had been clearly established. *The old girl* was no doubt my age, give or take a year or two, unless she happened to be among the few women in Argentina who marry late—after twenty-five, that is.

Freddy tries a final little number to test his widely-diffused brand of charm (that of the entire class of 1940, in other words). He takes me in his arms, and I don't defend myself. I note with pride that it's not a courtesy embrace. I feel his desire grow against my hopeless frigidity. I don't like this boy. I don't like boys young enough to be my sons, which I regret, because it destines me for a solitary old age and this disoriented maturity. I let him go off toward his planned, sensible destiny: the fiancée four years younger, from the same social circle, the father-in-law who will put him on the Board of Directors of two or three of his companies, the previously arranged civil and religious wedding ceremonies (although they consider themselves very modern and free because they have not waited for the bishop's blessing before making love). Suddenly it seems to me that all human beings are like the little crabs who scurry in different directions when I lift up a rock and look at them with *my* eyes, which to them are the eyes of God. I wonder if God, his mind on other matters, is casting an indifferent gaze at our scattered and incoherent movements.

January 1

New Year's Eve, and the reappearance of an old love. Last night I saw Rolando appear at Humberto's party. He looked wonderful, in a yellow T-shirt (yellow becomes him), deeply tanned, with that cheerful expression he usually adopts at large gatherings. I always fool myself and think he is capable of being equally jovial in private. It is strange, but in matters of love one's own experience isn't any more useful than that of others. Every time Rolando tried to initiate a romance with me, everything ended in a vulgar, awkward fashion after a few weeks, amidst a tide of mutual reproaches, well-aimed barbs, insults, and the mutual certainty that we had relapsed into hopeless misunderstanding. But neither of us really knows how to find another hanging tree.

He came from Punta del Este unannounced. Since the hotel was almost totally shut down for repairs, I offered to drive him to La Pedrera. Naturally he took offense. He said that since he had come all this way on my account he should be put up at my house for two or three nights. I claimed that at any moment Alejandra was coming for a visit and that, it being New Year's Day, maybe Iván, Dolores, and Alejo would be dropping in. He branded me prudish, old-fashioned, and hypocritical, and said disdainfully that my prejudices took away my personality. Actually, right then I had neither prejudices nor personality. I just wanted to be alone.... I knew that Rolando and I could only endure each other or tear each other to pieces, but that neither of us was the answer for the other's life. What's more, I have observed that for each man we lack personality or abound in prejudices when we are not doing what is in his interest. We drank a lot, and we ate a sort of bouillabaisse, a specialty of Humberto's. Rolando had three helpings. I whispered that seafood usually didn't agree with him. His look was withering. At three a.m. he got into my car, where we had put his bag. He said, "That wasn't real whiskey. I have heartburn." He added, "The champagne was undrinkable." I knew the bouillabaisse would be next. And so it was: "That concoction wasn't anything like bouillabaisse. It was an ordinary stew, and the seafood wasn't even fresh. I have a soccer ball in my stomach."

With resignation, I headed for *La Barcaza*. Rolando set himself up in the guest room, opened his suitcase and took out a tin of caviar, a bottle of French champagne, packs of cigarettes, marrons glacés, everything he was able to purchase on the boat. He offered them to me triumphantly. "Tomorrow we'll start the new year with all this, and not with the poison they gave us today." I thanked him effusively but knew that in the morning he would wake up with hives and blame me for having let him eat seafood.

This morning we went to the beach. Because he had hives, Rolando did not take off his T-shirt. I swam by myself for a long while until Nino joined me, as he does almost every morning. We stepped out of the water together. Nino told Rolando he ought to take a dip, that the water was splendid. I started to say he was suffering from hives, but Rolando cut me off. He told Nino he had never in his life had hives, that he was one of those rare people who had never suffered from any kind of seafood poisoning, but that he detested the calm, peaceful waters of La Aguada and we would be taking a dip at Solari later. We pulled up the beach umbrella, gathered our belongings, and headed for the car downcast, our individual storms brewing.

"Why was it necessary to say I had hives?" Well, I thought, the first drops are starting to fall. The clouds are building up, the thunder is rolling, and the lightning is flashing. We're like two fighting cocks. Each one of us is outfitted with razors capable of inflicting mortal wounds. Slowly we began advancing on the path of insults and recriminations. It is terrible when a man and a woman look at each other as if they're looking into a mirror which reflects back their own failures. I thought: "Rolando, go away, go away as soon as possible. My solitude is a victory; our being together is a failure." Maybe he had similar thoughts.

As I had predicted he told me to save all the delicacies for entertaining more cheerful friends. We ate boiled rice and stewed peaches.

Now I hear him walking back and forth in search of the starch, although I explained quite clearly that it was in the one green cabinet in the kitchen. He returns so he can tell me there's no starch in the white cabinets. I repeat that it is in the green cabinet. He says there's no green cabinet in the kitchen. I doubt it has vanished into thin air. I accompany him, I point to the green cabinet and ask if he suffers from color blindness. He says, "It's not green; it's blue." But he takes possession of the starch and goes to run his bath. He asks if I have any antihistamines or bicarbonate. Yes, of course, I have everything.

I know he will blame me because the typewriter I'm writing this diary with has kept him from napping in spite of the fact he didn't sleep a wink last night from the itching. That surprises me, because I went to wake him up at noon today and he was snoring steadily. But Rolando never admits in private that he has slept eight hours, nor in public that he has heartburn. I've always wondered how truthful he is when alone face to face with himself. Does he confess he spent a peaceful night? Is he diabolically cheerful about having tormented me when he says he is suffering from serious poisoning or an incipient heart attack? Does he laugh at himself, at me, at others, at everyone, at no one? Never could I drag out of him who he was according to his own estimate. Never could I find out if he was suffocating in the midst of a daily life filled with distractions and tasks deliberately assumed; if the office, roulette, golf, call-girl parties, the lengthy business dinners with his brothers (where their plans never amount to much) were just so many ways of stifling his impossible aspirations to heroism, sainthood or creativity, as he would have me believe; or if they were simply the truth of his life. Maybe he aspired to another kind of life but couldn't visualize it, because of a complete lack of imagination. My life was always inhabited by men with more than enough imagination. Santiago even built a raft and a hut like Robinson Crusoe, and we were ready to be shipwrecked...this was many years ago. Others would tell fortunes with cards or read palms. We tried witchcraft, we practiced spiritualism. In the port district we found cabarets where black and Japanese prostitutes hung out. Some of these imaginative men played the guitar or the accordion. They knew extraordinary parlor games brought from the United States. Together we would decorate walls with blue sirens and violet octopi. They couldn't make love on hot February nights. We used to find incunables in the second-hand book stores on Corrientes Street. We raised white rabbits on the roof. We grew tarragon in a pot, for making sauces and enjoying meals with a Parisian touch. Fabricio knew the ballads of Spain by heart and frank off-color stories we hadn't heard before. In what world did I meet these imaginative men who could change even the color of the air? In that of youth perhaps, in the days of ardent desire, insatiable and triumphant sex. And from what world did Rolando come? From that of my fatigue, perhaps, from the world which makes me shrug my shoulders in response to Nino's impertinent attentions and Freddy's determinedgallantry.

With Dickie we'd always talk in rhymes, but jokingly, and we'd laugh and laugh, oh Lord, how we used to laugh! How long has it been since I've laughed? Months, years? I don't know. Sometimes I cry a little, but not much. I fear I'm turning to stone.

Rolando opens the door a crack. He tells me he's better and feels like taking a walk, that it's completely impossible to sleep in this house with my damned typewriter clacking.

I'm going out too. I want to go up to the hotel and phone Dolores to wish them a Happy New Year. Mine is already off to a bad start. But then my new years are more and more the same old thing. I think enviously of Nickie and Facundo, who are still living in the fullness of imagination. Alejandra too, maybe; but her lover is likely to be a dull fellow more and more caught up in the mess of a divorce which is impossible, because his wife does not want it. He must talk incessantly of alimony and community property. Alejandra—I know her—will tell him to let his wife have it all, and they will remake their life together, with what she earns.... Poor Alejandra, who still doesn't understand anything. Suddenly I have a terrible longing to see her, to know the whole truth. Rolando is furiously beeping the horn. Apparently he doesn't feel as much like walking as he said he did. I'm coming, I'm coming....

January 3

Today I began to remember all manner of things from the past, just like a drowning person (so they say—I've never drowned). I remember Dickie's parlor games. The essential question: how many men can a decent woman have in her lifetime? Dickie...now I remember we used to call him Diquecito. That was a way of making the name Argentinean and affectionately overdoing the diminutive. Let's see now...how many? Ten...twelve, fourteen.... We would laugh.... Don't overdo it, not so many.... Eight...nine.... Yes...that is, it depends on what you mean by men. I mean something which should be fairly clear, leaving aside daddies and brothers, except in unexpected cases of incest (laughter), sons, domestic animals: how many men—in the active sense—does a decent woman have in her lifetime? And male friends, platonic boy friends? we would insist hypocritically, playing for time. Then Diquecito would turn serious. Don't force me to say *studs,* because that is nasty, isn't it? Then we women would turn serious, too. Don't get mad, Diquecito. More than one. Of course. More than two. Well, almost certainly. More than three?... Look, that depends.... Four. Yes, possibly. If all the women there were scarcely older than thirty, how could we know about the men who might come later? Four, five. Accepted. Diquecito died a senseless, awful death. Some gangsters intercepted him on a country road at night. Because he was coming from the dairy cooperative and had to pay the percentages and salaries, they thought he was carrying money. He was a cheerful person, bright and full of imagination, and nobody remembers him but me, as I try to recall his parlor games and that Roman gladiator's distaste with which he would make love, always at nap time. Any other hour seemed to him "mama and papa" style. Incidentally, Rolando left. He says he is going to return for another weekend and for *Carnaval.* It's all planned. Generously, he left behind the caviar, the champagne, and the cans of tea, tuna, sardines, and marrons glacés. He used just my bicarbonate and starch. This morning María was complaining. She needed the starch for my only pair of white pants. Never again will I buy white linen pants. But he left and it is as if I had escaped from a false destiny, comfortable and uncomfortable. What is bourgeois is always uncomfortable, in spite of claims to the contrary. Right, Diquecito? When Rolando is around I hide my palette and canvases for fear his remarks will make me fall from the tight rope every artist walks, which never has a safety net below.

January 7

I was ready to recount in lavish detail my Twelfth Night and the monotony of being available as grandmother on fixed occasions, when the door opened and the hotel boy handed me a telegram: Alejandra was arriving. I was stunned. The door opened again, and Alejandra—who had come on the same ONDA bus as the telegram—stood silhouetted in the doorway. We hugged effusively, if that word fits any of my second daughter's actions. Her skin and my skin don't go well together. Strange as it may seem, this is a phenomenon one notices not only with lovers, but with others to whom one is attached. I like to be affectionate with Nickie, but not with her sisters.

Alejandra left her bag and purse on the floor as if she expected a battalion of servants to rush in and carry them away. I picked up the handbag (of course I didn't touch the heavy suitcase) and showed her to her room. "This house is like an *amueblado*," I said, thinking of the kind of hotel where clandestine lovers meet: "People occupy this room by the hour." Alejandra took off a transparent rain jacket, the type worn by UFO flight crews, and followed me to the living room. She was not in a chatty mood, but it seemed inappropriate to offer to play lotto with her as I did when she was a little girl down with measles or a sore throat. A subject of conversation would have to be sought. Another of the obligations of the modern mother is to seek subjects of conversation.

They, most astute, do not talk. They let us get stuck in mud up to our necks and then leap on us. We are tactless, we are monstrous parents, we say to them everything one should not say. I know the basics: not to talk about myself, nor my problems, because they are not of the slightest interest; nor should I mention my male friends. Faced with the disapproving looks of daughters and sons-in-law, amid an atmosphere thick enough to cut with a knife, I must declare that the men I know are homosexual or impotent so my family does not assume they are all my lovers. It is also dangerous to mention my women friends. They're all sluts, they sleep with little boys. They have arteriosclerosis or are simply stupid and old-fashioned. I look for a subject of conversation, feeling my way along like a blind person. I know what's important is to talk to them about their precious persons, their precious things, their precious clothes, their houses—marvels of good taste—and about the miracles they manage to perform: sending their servant to the market, feeding their child, or earning their daily bread.

With Alejandra the main thing is to act dazzled by the exceptional position she holds at the United Nations, to complain mildly about her absence and about how I worry sometimes knowing she's so far away.... Ouch! I have fallen into her trap.

"And what do you want me to do here? Marry the first idiot that comes along, like Dolores and Nickie?"

"The truth is I have to contradict you, since many other idiots passed through both their lives. Let's say they married the tenth...."

She shrugs: "I never had a real home." "What is a real home?" I ask sweetly. "Well.... Papa went his way, and you went yours...."

"You don't remember. You were quite small when he died. Besides, he was in the navy. He couldn't sail around the bathtub. I too would have liked what you call a real home. The four of us weren't that miserable."

"For heaven's sake, Mama! You are blind."

"Like all mothers, and like all daughters."

"I didn't have any affection."

I look at her. Here she is—harsh, as disagreeable as a

porcupine. I remember her cutting words, her choice to live far away from me, her main excuse: to earn dollars and not devalued pesos. Affection! The word affection is always tumbling out of their calculating, greedy mouths.

I get up, fetch ice, and serve two whiskeys. This allows me to change the subject. I recount her godchild's charming antics. Yesterday we spent the day together. For his Twelfth Night gift, I gave him a bicycle which they placed on his shoes as if it had been brought by the Magi. His parents handed him their gifts personally. So they looked good, and grandmother felt embarrassed.

"Your godson is a dear, he has natural charm. Before, they'd use Alejandro; now they call him Alejo; it's shorter...."

"Dolores was always quite original," Alejandra says sarcastically.

I smile: "Alejo is a nice name. Sometimes Iván calls him Alexis."

"The child will end up not knowing *what* his name is."

"Don't you believe it. He is not at all dumb. He has the profound gaze of an adult. Sometimes he lowers his eyes as if he didn't want us to guess what he's thinking. No doubt he believes that all his thoughts can escape through his eyes. He believes he is transparent."

"All children think that. I was the same way at his age. What's going on is just that you never understood us."

Oh, dear! To which saint do I turn so as not to touch upon subjects which allow her to stir up her ancient, renewed resentments? How is it that two years in the United States didn't smooth out her rough edges? Often, being far away makes us idealize those left behind in the land of our birth...suddenly I understand. I have a little wounded animal in front of me. She has not arrived here on a whim. She has been fleeing from something. From what? How do I get her to talk without her spitting out insults? If our two skins went well together, if I could take her in my arms....

Alejandra goes on, "At least, you never understood *me*."

"Never?" I ask, remembering the nights she'd curl up in my

bed with Nickie.

"Maybe when I was very small, I don't know. But later, that's what's important. Of course, here life is so easy. Here you are spending four months at the seaside, like a queen...."

She seems to believe that La Paloma is my usual residence, that I am a siren gracefully aging on the shores of this deep, warm sea.

"Why like a queen?" I ask ingenuously, knowing my revenge is at hand. To know she expects a meal, one only has to see her voraciously eating the last little piece of cheese and scraping up the bits of left-over fried potatoes.

"It would be very good for Argentineans to spend a few months in the United States. They would find out what it means to manage completely on their own...."

She's not dumb. She senses she's wrong. She looks around at the closed and half-closed doors. She adds, rather meek: "Is it the maid's day out?"

"What maid?" I ask, relentlessly naïve.

"I don't know...but you always had a maid," she says, her voice firmer.

"What does *always* mean? Some years, yes, of course, when they didn't quit on me with you two screaming and Nickie in my belly...or with the three of you demanding your dinner, your toys...everything."

"Fine, except when they quit on you," she agrees with condescending irony, "you always had a maid."

"That's right. But everywhere on our planet life has changed. One doesn't have to move to the United States. In Moscow once they had czars. In Cuba too everything has changed."

"And in Argentina?"

"Right now we're in Uruguay. The people here are like Neapolitans. They think it's better to enjoy the sun rather than work such long hours, the way you do. All manners of looking at life are valid."

"I believe in work."

"So do I. That's why I'm inviting you to show me the cooking skills you acquired in the USA."

"Cooking never was my thing, but if you insist...."

"You've at least learned to open cans, haven't you? Because that's what I'm worst at: opening cans and uncorking bottles. Apart from that, I can make you a stuffed chicken, bass with roquefort, a Spanish omelet. Choose...."

She lowers her eyes, disconcerted. Her voice is fainter: "You don't have anybody?"

"Oh, yes, I do have a very likeable girl who washes and irons and straightens up, which she does from two to five on the days she's in the mood. She can't perform miracles."

"And in Buenos Aires?"

"I shall see. Micaela left because she had surgery for a polyp in her uterus. I fear it may be cancer. When I get back, I'll decide what to do. It would be stupid to ruin my summer thinking about domestic problems, wouldn't it?"

She looks at me. Through her eyes I can see a parade of white-gloved footmen, a row of maids wearing stiffly starched aprons and caps on their heads: her dreams in New York when remembering Argentina. She's my daughter, I love her and—in spite of her relentlessly passing judgment on her mother—I want her to have the best visit possible. Furthermore, I'm convinced she has a serious problem of the heart.

"Don't worry. I'm taking you to dinner at Humberto's restaurant. Because you came, it's a holiday."

I stroke her hair awkwardly, and she pulls her head away in spite of herself. It is not in my power nor in hers to create any affection between her skin and mine.

January 8

Alejandra unwound, ate, and drank. Humberto courted her as he does every woman who comes to his place. He is like a shipboard purser. His main duty is to keep the women coming back, to make them roll their eyes and sigh when they remember this great vessel known as La Paloma.

On the way home she recounted her drama, which she believes to be quite novel. She is in love with a married man who can't make up his mind about leaving his wife. Of course I was careful not to tell her that all up and down the Uruguayan and Argentinean coasts thousands of women were weeping for the same reason. She is the only one. For me she has to be, since she is my daughter.

"He's a beast," she says, "or he wouldn't have started seeing me, or he would have made up his mind right away and left Dorothy."

"And the community property and the alimony payments and the dubious Dunoyer de Segonzac...."

"It's an Othon Friezs," she says, amazed.

"And the Baccarat goblets, the Limoges china, the signed dresser and the record collection with the records neither of them ever listens to...."

"So you knew something about me and Bob?"

I smile and shrug my shoulders. I know so much about so many Bobs and about so many girls who think they are more valuable than art objects and well-appointed homes.

"Your letters made me suspect something," I say vaguely. "At any rate, I've just now found out his name is Bob."

"He is a beast," she repeats, obstinate because she's had one too many.

"Does he have any children?"

"One son in the diplomatic corps. He lives in Paris."

"He's considerably older than you," I state, showing how sharp I am.

"Not that much. Robert entered the service through Bob's connections. The truth is that he's just twenty years older than I am. He was a boy when he married. They trapped him because he got Dorothy pregnant."

Here we have history reconstructed. I feel more at ease.

"He's a beast," she repeats.

I think all women consider beasts the men who don't love them enough or who are in love with others. We don't know that they are weak, that their outstretched hands don't signify hands filled with gifts; instead they are the hands of beggars, empty, like ours. Any woman can lose a man, any other woman can win him, and a third can snatch him away from her. Plain truths experienced by countless generations of women who keep them quiet and do not pass them on to their daughters. We believe men are strong and we require of them the attributes of the strong, but everything becomes transparent as soon as we find out they are as weak as we women and as relentless. It is not the right moment to remind Alejandra that a weak man treats a woman as cruelly as a son does his mother. It's the only sphere where he knows he's strong, the sphere of another's love, a love which has been aroused without his deserving it. A strong man believes himself much weaker than he is, a weak man believes himself much stronger. His weakness makes him the woman's equal and thus her adversary. One tests one's mettle with one's equals, never with superiors or inferiors.

Casually, I ask her: "What are your plans?"

"I don't know.... I've requested a leave of absence for now. I could stay here half the time, the other half at Dolores' house...she offered," she adds quickly.

I feel like slapping her. Does she care whether she causes me problems or not? How does she know if I'm living alone or if there's a man in my life? Did it occur to her to ask me why I've ended up burying myself here amid these vast stretches of salt and sand? No, it didn't occur to Dolores and Nickie either. No one has delved into my motives, no one. To Alejandra, it seemed natural to go abroad "forever and ever." My solitude was not her problem then and isn't now.

A heavy silence settles between us. A silence which affects her like a cold shower and evaporates the alcohol fumes.

"You can stay a few days," my tone is neutral. "Also, you can go to my apartment in Buenos Aires. It's empty. You'll be very comfortable."

The available mother is not rebelling but slowly and deliberately making her conditions clear. Is this what I have a mother for? Alejandra must be thinking, disgusted with the world, with Bob, and with me. So is this what I'm stuck with: a lover who can't make up his mind about leaving his wife, a mother who is not at my disposal, a planet I can't bounce up and down like a ball on a string? What a disappointment.

"Would you like another whiskey before you turn in?" I ask her, indicating it is bedtime.

"No, thanks." She stands up. She kisses my forehead. "We'll talk tomorrow. I might have to go to Buenos Aires for a few days. Here it's like the ends of the earth. I can't be so out of touch...."

"Of course not. Did you give Bob my phone number there?"

"Yes."

"And for letters?"

"I arranged to telegraph him. I'll do it tomorrow. That reminds me, I came with very little money so I wouldn't have to exchange dollars...there's a devaluation every week in these countries down here."

"Let's not exaggerate...."

"Since you're getting Papa's entire pension...."

"Daughters who have reached their majority do not get any pension benefits...I believe."

"You're wrong. They only lose them when they marry...."

"Ah! Maybe I am wrong. I know they can be claimed in cases of indigence, disability, old age, or if the adult daughter had been supported by the father. But it's true I know little about these things. Anyway, if you need something...laws don't matter."

She replies abruptly, "I don't need anything." Then why is she asking, I wonder.

"I told you it's just for the first few days. After that I'll have a withdrawal made. I have an account in dollars at a New York bank." And in what other currency can one have an account at a New York bank?

Heartily, I say, "For Heaven's sake, child, it's not a problem."

But, once again the split dividing us has grown deeper. In this new world they want to create to their liking, young people will not abandon the concept that mothers are available in the same way Chartres Cathedral and the frescoes in the Sistine Chapel are available. This concept in no way implies that the young must respect these human ruins and do not have an inalienable right to paint over black and white surfaces with red and green stripes or polka dots. We mothers are under an obligation to remain standing, as solid and available as Gothic cathedrals; but we also have an obligation to be dazzled by the stupidities our children reveal in passing so as to astonish us. I too was a daughter. That's why I am being kind.

January 9

At ten after twelve I went into Alejandra's room. She was dozing, not really sleeping.

"It's a lovely day," I said. "Get up. Let's go to the beach."

"Your maid didn't come?" she asked.

I realized that, in accordance with the child-parent relationship, she had not heard my explanation of the night before. She had arrived on Latin American soil eager for breakfast in bed.

"She comes at two; but if you like, I'll bring you some tea. It's made. I've already had mine."

She smiled. I left, and when I returned with the tray, she sat up and said happily, "How marvelous it is to have breakfast in bed."

Right then the doorbell rang. I don't know if it is a fate peculiar to me, but if I have two phones, both will ring at the same time. If I am going to initiate an earth-shaking conversation, every sound-producing device in the house will ring at once: phones, doorbell, alarm clock.

It was the delivery boy from the grocery, bringing an order from three days ago. Time passes in its own fashion here.

January 10

Alejandra is taking up much of my day, and I can't even paint.

I've already introduced her to my friends. In general, they made a good impression, except for Nino. He considers her a stuck-up creature, and she considers him a country hick. Could this be the beginning of a great love? In the arms of a La Paloma fisherman's son, could she forget her deathless love for a North American banker?

As we bicycled along the road to La Aguada this afternoon I asked her, "How in the world did you happen to get involved with a married man?"

"They have divorce there," she claimed as an excuse.

"But that's just the reason *not* to get involved," I insisted. "In countries where divorce is non-existent the legal wife has no protection at all. Forming a secret partnership is all that's needed to leave her in poverty; but in countries where there is divorce, the laws, society, everything conspires against the interloper."

She gave me a surprised look. "Something like that is happening," she muttered. "There women form a clan, a freemasonry. Here they do each other in."

"Haven't you met any boys your own age?"

"Men my age don't exist."

That's true, I thought; they don't. There are never men our age, the right age. They're either too young or too old. I did some calculations in my head. They couldn't have died in the Second World War. I told her so.

"And the Vietnam War?" she replied.

"Oh, of course."

But that's not the reason," she said, exasperated, as if she were being forced to carry on a conversation with a complete fool. "It's just that there's an age when men have a quiet home life with wife and children because they have things more important to do than look for love."

Shocked, I said, "There's nothing more important than love."

"Maybe that was so in your day. Today it's a pastime left for old age, like golf and bridge. Now they have to make money."

"Aha!" I said in a stupid tone.

"...and when they acquire their money they'll do what Bob is doing with me. They will look for a great love and they won't dare divorce because it ends up being too expensive to be funny."

I venture an opinion: "It seems to be a rather poorly organized generation."

Unquestionably, making money does take time. While Alejandra was talking, I thought of many Argentinean Bobs who were like the Bobs of the North. Greedily, covetously, they amass that money to be enjoyed by a widow after their premature heart attacks; they may give up more than half of it so that true love can at last become part of their life; or the money may be what keeps that love from becoming part of their life. But obviously these are the silly thoughts one has in a place like La Paloma where there are no shops, theatres, nightclubs, de luxe restaurants, no sense of competition, no feverish atmosphere. A boring paradise where one can think, like a philosopher from another century.

We went to The Magic Seashell for the evening. Humberto was in a strangely excited state. He had just seen a flying saucer and could not wait on anyone. He was attempting to reproduce on canvas the monster which had just crossed our skies. According to him, these saucers are not space vehicles but beings different from us, something like giant flying tortoises. One of them can take a man, a car, a house, and transport them anywhere it pleases.

Almost all of La Paloma's summer visitors had arranged to meet at Humberto's night club. The French couple was there. These two make love at night on the sand. While they are completing this task, they either ignore passersby or greet them with a friendly wave. There are a Belgian diplomat and his spouse, extremely proper, the parents of seven little darlings whose mere presence justifies the behavior of Herod. These children are totally unlike their parents and burst into dinner parties (if the hosts have forgotten to lock their doors) shouting like Indians and brandishing lighted torches. They invade the hotel hallways and the beach, where they spend a few minutes indifferently observing the ardent, unperturbed French couple. The parents believe that all South

American children are insufferable and that consequently they ought not to train their own children lest the little darlings become misfits. On a few occasions I have initiated a mild discussion on this subject, something to the effect that "there are all kinds of ways...in child raising, too, there are subtle little differences," but they don't listen to reason. That night, as we surrounded the inspired Humberto (when we arrived he was placing on his UFO the head of a tortoise with whale-like jaws) five of the seven little Van der Berghs, in diving costumes, were masquerading as creatures who had just stepped out of the space vehicle. This disturbed Humberto's painting and theorizing to such an extent that he, so gentle by nature, turned around and, to the surprise of the spectators, kicked the children several times. Then he went on painting, first ordering the crowd of spectators, "Take all the chairs and tables outdoors. Don't distract me. This is the discovery of the century."

The Van der Berghs tended to the wailing of their shocked children, and everyone began to bandy about his or her own theory of child raising.

"*Sale métèque...espèce de sauvage*," Mrs. Van der Bergh was muttering.

Hereupon Alejandra began speaking, with the flat intonation which distinguishes those who have passed through that school of moderation and patience known as the United Nations. She stated that children's forms of amusement should not be repressed. Such repression gives rise to the complexes which in later years produce frustrated men; on the other hand, if children are allowed to burn down the neighbors' houses, in years to come they will be healthy men and women, useful to society.

The Van der Berghs were looking at her, entranced. I said I could not accept a world populated with sterile, psychoanalyzed creatures, healthy and flourishing amid the ashes of the houses they had burned down as children, a world without Mallarmé, Rimbaud, Poe, or Dosteovsky.

"Do you think training a child is all it takes to turn him into a genius?"

"I think not training him is all it takes to turn him into an idiot," I said irritably.

I then left the scene, determined not to let myself be taken in by the social life of La Paloma. I had come here to look for solitude and to find myself, not to belong to a group whose social activities were less expensive than Punta del Este's.

Instead of getting in my car, I went deep into the woods. I don't enjoy walking and am not very good at vertical movement, but I do like strolling under the pines, bending down to pick up a pine cone, breathing in air which is transformed by the mere presence of trees. I needed to forget the UFO, the Van der Bergh children, Alejandra, and my whole family, which knows nothing about me and asks so much of me.

Suddenly it occurred to me I had not heard from Papa since November. He was probably at his little apartment in Portofino as usual, with the charming woman (my age) who is his companion, to whom he has little to give while alive and much less after he dies, since his worldly goods have come down to an ambassador's abundant retirement check, and they have been unable to marry. Her husband still lives on Argentinean soil. I felt depressed. The world seemed to me poorly organized, a fact which is indisputable whatever our state of mind, and I told myself that if the invasion of my house by visitors did not stop soon, the only way for me to be alone would be to return to Buenos Aires. I wanted to write my study of Manet, but my ideas were floating away, partly from the drowsiness brought on by sun and sea, but mostly because of disturbing presences. The worst was Alejandra's. How long would she be here? What right did she have to consider me available, she who had decided to settle down abroad to fulfill her destiny and was now obstructing mine? I had always accepted my daughters' independence, their personalities, their whims, but I was beginning to realize that without a second thought they were trying to turn me into an available mother. They were taking me by surprise, putting a bonnet on my head and knitting needles in my hands, the way straightjackets are put on mental patients. But my hearing was keen, and I heard them approach in spite of their bare feet and their fluid, drowning-victim movements. Now I am determined. I am going to talk with Alejandra. I am going to ask what her plans are, how long she intends to stay, how much vacation she has. If it is going to stretch on, I'll make her think I'm expecting my lover.

Once I had made these decisions, I went back inside The Magic Seashell, now free of Belgian redskins. Curious, I took a look at the flying tortoise.

"How does it strike you?" Humberto asked me.

"How does what strike me, the drawing or the theory?"

"Both."

"The drawing is just for illustrating the theory, I assume?"

"Of course."

I do not want to annoy Humberto, not only because he extended me his warm hospitality from the very first, but because he is attractive and would be truly attractive if he didn't believe himself under an obligation to paw every female newcomer, the way they beat up on the new boys at school.

"Did you really see the UFO?"

"Nino saw it too."

"Ah, then it's serious," I said in a serious tone.

Humberto burst out laughing.

"Apparently you have more faith in Nino than in me."

"Nino does not have enough imagination to lie, nor does he need to promote himself."

"Don't believe it. Maybe this is our way of attracting tourists."

"Where is Alejandra?" I asked, looking around the room.

"I don't know...she was here a while ago, having a lively conversation with Van der Bergh."

I shuddered. I too have my theories, as valid as Humberto's theory about giant extraterrestrial tortoises. There are women who never become involved with a married man; others set their sights only on married men. Don't ask me why, for I don't know the causes. That's just the way it is. Maybe I'm lying when I say I don't know the causes. I simply have not concerned myself with delving deeply into the problem, but I am sure that behavior like Alejandra's arises from an impossible love for the father or from unrestrained contempt for other women. It is a question of an unhealthy, uncontrollable passion and a hate-filled sense of justice and equality, similar to that of communists: by what right are you rich while I am poor? By what right do you have a man of your own while I have none? This fits in quite well with Alejandra's character. She is obsessed with justice and that is, of course, how she sows injustice all around her. She is in a sense the standard for her world, but others do not use her as the measure for their actions. Moreover, let's not forget her four years of translating speeches about hunger in underdeveloped countries, disease caused by malnutrition, man's greatness in confronting his ignoble fate, the certainty of raising (thanks to these high-level meetings) the low level of the rest of the planet's inhabitants. Such years would leave their mark on anyone, and even more so on someone as impressionable as Alejandra. Generally men have more faith in words than deeds, and women more faith in deeds than words. In this area, Alejandra is clearly somewhat masculine. She firmly believes what they tell her. Thus, she is the ideal prey for married men. What married man, when he has downed two or three whiskeys, does not warmly confide in the pretty woman at his side that all is not happiness in his household, that his wife doesn't understand him, that she became frigid after the third child was born or after she had her tonsils out? To make a long story short, both he and the pretty girl agree completely on all these points. It terrifies me to think Alejandra may want to console herself with this Belgian embassy attaché over the disappointment occasioned by what she calls "Bob's lack of character." That is all I need for my summer vacation to end up completely ruined.

When I arrived at the house Alejandra had not yet come in. I went to bed and busied myself reading. After ten pages I became aware that absolutely nothing had sunk in, that I was thinking only about the indiscretions Alejandra was probably committing. I'm an idiot, I told myself. My daughters are adults, let them get by on their own. I have a right to live my life, as they themselves would say. And to affirm that right, I took a sedative and went to sleep. I didn't hear her come in. She says she returned at three a.m. Today for certain I'm going to talk to her and establish my right to solitude. They give me nothing, I ask them for nothing, except to leave me in peace.

January 11

I woke up determined to make my rights prevail. It was a splendid day. We are in the midst of a drought. Evidently it has not rained here for three months. The farmers are alarmed, the summer visitors overjoyed. Just like an ordinary person, God is thinking that you can't please everybody. I pushed open my wooden shutters and gazed at the sea below. I'd like to be able to sit for two or three hours gazing at the sea in summer or at the fire in winter, not asking any more from life nor trying to contribute anything more to it. But unfortunately I am an active beast. A lion is not a lizard. It is useless to go against nature. For ten minutes which seemed like two hours, I enjoyed the blue sea and the sun playing on the moving water. Then, my limited thirst for contemplation quenched, I went to the kitchen to make breakfast. The door to Alejandra's room was shut. In a sudden burst of anger I thought of how she had not lifted a finger yet in spite of her measured, enlightening speeches on the obligation to be self-sufficient. I had taken her breakfast in bed several times. Today she would have to manage on her own. I'm sick and tired of the United States, I said to myself angrily. Here we do the same thing without making such a fuss.

After downing two cups of tea and a cracker, I put on a bathing suit and stretch fabric overalls, scribbled a few lines to tell Alejandra I was on going to Bahía Chica for a dip, was taking the car and would leave her the bicycle.

I need to be a part of something in order to love it. The sea was even more exquisite surrounding my body than when seen from my window. Nino appeared beside me suddenly, but I can't say unexpectedly, since his presence is already as predictable as that of the tiny crabs among the rocks. We swam a while, either silent or exchanging broken-up phrases about Humberto and the UFO. Evidently he had been so entranced that he planned to change the name of his nightclub and call it The Tortoise from Outer Space. I told Nino the name would be amusing for a few days but after that would suggest nothing, since no one would remember the sighting of the supposed flying saucer or Humberto's theory. "Why don't we suggest to him that it could be an octopus, not a tortoise, and that perhaps it has tentacles?" I said. We laughed and swam toward the beach.

"And your daughter?... She's gone?" asked Nino when he saw I was alone under my beach umbrella.

"No, I think she's sleeping, or she might have gone to Solari. She's already made several friends here."

"Is she planning to spend the whole summer with you?"

"Oh, good heavens, no!" I exclaimed in spite of myself.

Nino smiled faintly. He is most tactful and thought, not without reason, that I would prefer to avoid comments about my exclamation.

At two-thirty I decided to go back home. Alejandra's absence was worrying me. Of all the occupations, motherhood is the most infernal. Once a certain stage in the lives of children and parents is reached, all that remains is worrying about the dangers our absent children may encounter and becoming impatient (and mastering our impatience) in face of that arrogant passing of judgement which their presence entails. Alejandra had left a note at home, informing me she was going to see her sister because she had a ride to Punta del Este and that she would undoubtedly be back by dark. It might have been a last-minute invitation because she left her bed only partly made, her clothes strewn about, and, unusual for her, the closet door open. I asked María to straighten up Alejandra's room, and I found myself faced with an empty day...that day, so longed for, coming to me so suddenly now, seemed meaningless.

I missed Rolando's presence. He at least was there even if he did sleep fourteen hours on the pretext he had not had a wink of sleep all night, and even if he did use up all the starch intended for the sheets so he could soothe the hives caused by shellfish, "which never causes him hives."

I begin preparing my canvas, using the infallible method taught me by a painter friend who lived in Florence for several years. One of the secrets of my success is having learned that preparing the canvas is as important as preparing the paints, and I take great care over this seemingly unimportant and unknown task. While carrying out this manual chore I feel as if I possess the secrets of the alchemist. And my mind can hover around the matters worrying me. The accumulated years still rest lightly on my shoulders, but one day I'll suddenly feel their weight in a joint or vertebra and will be fully aware of time's destructiveness.

What has this nearly half century on earth given me? And I, what have I given? I think that if the world had given me more, I would have given it back threefold. But I am among those people never on the right side, whose windows the sun pours into at noon in midsummer and barely touches in winter. I am among those who arouse suspicion in the official world whatever its makeup at the time in which they happen to live; moreover, my spine is too stiff. I cannot bend over and pick up sinecures. I might have been born a man. I sigh...I agree with the existentialists that there is no *might have been.* Also, I *might have had* brothers, brothers-in-law, influential lovers, someone to claim for me on my behalf the position I could have occupied with efficiency and brilliance. I had no such men. My independent spirit arouses resistance. Because of that must I live without ambitions or change them into inner aspirations? I believe I actually did the latter: success and money faded away, and I ended up with arrogance and freedom. The balance sheet of my life is positive. I am proud of being myself. I don't know if many people can say as much.

Sometimes I would like to know how my daughters see me

and how they will see me after I'm dead. I deserve their love, but love is not obtained through merit.

My canvas is ready, and I'm thinking of going out to paint. There are some little boats at the marina which tempt me. It would be futile. Today I might do better sketching some of Alejandra's fleeting expressions. I can't stop thinking about her and that last-minute impulse to go see her sister. How can I manage to find out if she went with the Belgian diplomat? This shouldn't be too hard. His seven redskins must be out devastating the area, and if I buy them candy they will answer my questions.

I showered, put on a blouse and pants, took my market basket and went out to stroll around La Paloma.

I didn't have to go very far. The bakery delivery boy, tied to a tree, was trying to make his cries for help audible, while the seven Van der Berghs danced around a circle of burning newspapers, singing what were supposed to be native war chants but were actually stanzas of *La Madelon*. I approached them. The children were stunned. I live in a rather deserted spot, and they thought no one would come upon them in these parts.

Addressing the oldest one in a severe tone, I said, "I'm going to your papa right this minute and tell him all about you."

"Papa's not here. He's gone to Punta del Este," he replied.

"Then I'll tell your mama."

"Mama went to Punta del Este too. They went to a cocktail party...just like your daughter."

I've never seen such quick detective work. Going as a threesome did not decrease Alejandra's amorous risks, but at least it created one less problem for me with La Paloma's tourist population.

I did a little shopping, read a while and went to finish up the evening at The Magic Sea Shell, of which only the first and half of the second word remained—The Mag—because Humberto was covering over the rest.

I shouted in greeting, "The name of a boat must never be changed. It brings bad luck."

"This is not a boat. Besides, I'm not getting rid of it; I'm redoing it."

"What? Weren't you going to call it The Tortoise from Outer Space?"

"That name is a little long." And he added, not looking at me, "They tell me that it was not a UFO; it was a test balloon sent up by an atmospheric research commission."

"I am sorry," I said with the tone of someone offering condolences.

Humberto finished the word "Magic" and came down from the ladder.

"I'll do the rest tomorrow. It's a nuisance to paint under artificial light. I'd rather chat with you."

It was early and we were alone. I looked at my watch. A quarter to nine, and nobody would be coming here before ten. Suddenly my presence took on the meaning that intimacy was called for. What was I to do? The most sensible thing would be to resign myself to having the affair he was seeking; after all, he was a pleasant man, and there was no reason to consider it a tragedy. The only inconvenience would be the possible consequences of an affair in a place where I'd be staying for at least two more months. We know how an affair starts but not how it ends, I told myself candidly. The truth is, an hour later my thought was that we don't know how one starts, either.

Humberto took me inside, kissed me, and we fell awkwardly onto the sofa. His head struck the wall and although he said "It's nothing," I noticed he was in pain. He stuck an elbow right in the rib which has bothered me ever since I broke it in an automobile accident two years ago. We rolled about with the elegance of two seals who dream they are sirens. The cushions were full of lumps and hollows, thanks to the couples who curl up on them nightly to drink wine and sing French songs and tangos. Humberto kissed my mouth, unbuttoned my blouse, and kissed my breasts, while I (the real me, that is), freed from my earthly form, looked down with an ironic gaze upon this fiftyish pair pretending they wanted to make love. Nothing. Useless to thrash about, utter dirty words, to ask for my pitiful assistance. It was like giving Alejo a bath.

"It's the damned UFO," he muttered, admitting defeat. "I can't stand making a fool of myself."

Since it's twice in two days, I said to myself, you couldn't ask for a better record. I also thought about how my freshly ironed pants now looked like an accordion and how María wouldn't be coming until Monday. Humberto unlatched the door. The two of us looked toward the horizon and waited for the arrival of a patron, as nervous as Christopher Columbus when America stubbornly refused to loom up out of the waters.

January 12

Another glorious day, blue sky, unchanging sun. I was getting ready to go to the beach. First, as if to wipe out the memory of last night's fiasco, I meticulously ironed my sailcloth pants and flowered blouse. I wavered a minute or two about the notebook I had in my hand. It would be smart to take it to the beach, look through it there, try to recall what had inspired some of my notes, and add others. Maybe last night's experience.

No, that's universal, but on second thought, everything is universal. Even the metric system has taken over on the only island which rejected it. UFOs which are not UFOs, affairs which are not affairs, revolutions which are not revolutions, inflation which is not inflation because everything goes up more or less at the same time—it always ends up the same; in short, there's nothing new under the sun. Whether it's one old story or another, may the sun take pleasure in burning my arms and legs so at least no one will doubt that I have vacationed to the point of frenzy.

Just when I was about to leave, I heard a vehicle stop. I ran to the door and saw Iván's car and pouring out of it, all the members of the perfect family: Alejandra, smiling and looking maternal with Alejandro in tow; Dolores, Iván; and Iván's mother, my charming fellow mother-in-law, who is eager to report to Punta del Este in sordid detail my household arrangements, the reasons for my voluntary retreat, the kind of life I'm leading here.

Yet, when I saw Marina stepping out of Iván's car, I wondered why in the world she was coming to these parts. We are friends from childhood, but at eighteen we stopped seeing each other, and we remembered our friendship when our children became engaged. Like me, Marina belongs to a family of Argentinean gentry, but she also married gentry and has never deviated from her very proper path; what's more, since she is elegant, pretty, and wears clothes well (those quality clothes that aren't hard to wear) I find her presence overwhelming.

"What in the world made you come and bury yourself here?" she asked.

Astounded, I looked at her. She was the first person to show an interest in what had motivated me. Taken unawares, I babbled: "I need a little solitude. I want to finish my study of Manet and paint some landscapes."

But Marina is too simple to believe simple excuses which any complicated person would believe without batting an eye.

"Come on," she said with a laugh, "Don't tell *me* tales. Besides, you're so brown, it's obvious you're spending your time on the beach. Admit it...."

Her smile of complicity filled me with happiness. That very night all Punta del Este—my friends, their husbands, their lovers, their pseudohusbands, and pseudolovers—would firmly believe I was living a grand passion in La Paloma. All those wrinkled bodies, all those masses of cellulite covered with the illustrious marquis' designs, would suddenly be picturing my rejuvenated body, my evaporated cellulite, my firm neck, my unlined forehead, resting against the shoulder of a strong and mysterious stranger.

"I admit it," I said with a smile.

Dolores came up. Intrigued, she asked, "What are you two plotting?"

"Your mother-in-law is trying to convince me to go spend a weekend in Punta del Este and abandon myself to the delights of civilization."

Marina and I laughed while an unenthusiastic Dolores offered the opinion that one place was as good as another.

January 13

I spent an exhausting day. I had to sing the praises of La Paloma. We strolled in a congenial group, and a dozen times I had to avoid a dozen sticky subjects. The one that came up most often was Alejandra's stay: how happy I must be to have her here, what good company for me, how I would miss her when she left! Was this an order? Had she asked her sister to force me to keep her here? I was infuriated. The available mother, the Plaza San Marcos, the Leaning Tower of Pisa, Chartres Cathedral—with economy fares purchased on the installment plan, you can visit them whenever you're in the mood. After it's over, let the decaying, tottering old stones waste away alone; after all, we have a photo of ourselves standing next to them and smiling, a pigeon on our shoulder and several more at our feet. "*Merde, merde, trois fois merde*," I mumbled to myself in French since I'm more accustomed to using the word in that language than in Spanish, but obviously I did not say it very loud.

At last they left, while Alejandra and I stood waving goodbye. Then we went inside. I shut the door and, determined to plunge ahead, settled into an armchair and spoke severely: "Well now, we've had enough clowning. Where did you go, with whom, and why?"

"To Punta del Este with the Van der Berghs. I spent the night at Dolores' and I came back. What's so unusual about that?"

"What's unusual is that I have come here to be alone and untroubled so I can work on a book and that I have as much right as you to decide when I want to be alone and when I want company, and if you don't wish to go back to New York, I'm offering you my apartment in Buenos Aires for the months you're here, but I am expecting Juan."

I didn't utter that short name in a decisive tone but let it slide out slowly from between my lips as if caressing it.

"Who is Juan?"

"My lover."

At the time no more original name occurred to me, but just plain Juan turned out to be quite acceptable.

"How long is Juan staying?"

"Is that any of your business? The truth is that he's about to arrive, and I need your room for him."

"If he's your lover, I don't see why he doesn't sleep in your bed."

I looked at her, astounded, without finding a single word to reply.

"I like sleeping alone," I said finally.

"Then what is it you want a lover for?"

"To make use of him when I am awake."

Tit for tat, I said to myself, noticing that this time I had succeeded in shocking her.

"Fine, you're kicking me out, then."

"What other solution is there? I only have two bedrooms."

"I could sleep in the living room."

"You're joking."

My tone was too final for her to insist. A silence ensued in which I awaited filial reproaches. But Alejandra stood up, poured herself a shot of whiskey, measured soda as carefully as if it were laudanum, and did not utter a single word. Then I realized she was waiting for me to explain.

"Do I owe you an explanation?" I asked.

"I am not going to tell you your attitude is normal and is what I was expecting...." She was speaking in the deliberate, extremely polite and patient tone she had learned in that school of good manners known as the United Nations. "Every daughter thinks her arrival will fill her mother with joy."

"Every mother thinks the same," I interrupted abruptly, "and when I went to visit you in New York, you told me you were leaving for the Bahamas with a group of friends the very next day. You were on vacation. Incidentally, do you have eleven months of vacation a year?"

"No, but maybe I will, since I'm going to take advantage of this vacation to think things over. Deep down, I'm beginning to long for a bourgeois life, a husband, children, servants...."

"Not the servants again! An Argentinean can't go live abroad without believing he remembers that here we are waited on like Louis XIV."

"You always had very good maids. What's become of them?"

"Carmela was a jewel, but one day I went to her room and found her lover in his undershorts listening to a football game on the radio."

"And what did you do?"

"I told them that people who let themselves get caught are foolish and egotistical, because they complicate the lives of others. They married and complicated my life even more. Finally they left. They were about to have a baby, and they went to set up housekeeping on her father's farm. After that I hired another one, a gem, according to the woman at the agency, but the day before she was to start they put her in jail for assaulting her previous employer. In short, I'll spare you these boring domestic stories. At the moment I'm without anyone, but I'll see to it when I get back."

"The world has grown complicated," she said philosophically, but then added, "Basically you never learned how to deal with servants."

I wondered if accusations would begin coming in through the service entrance. But Alejandra is too smart not to have foreseen the reply on the tip of my tongue. No doubt she also wanted to avoid maternal reproaches, the immortal phrase "they leave me as alone as a dog," when in all the streets of the world dogs are always accompanied and human beings are often alone. She simply said, "Sometimes I feel a little sorry for you because you don't love anybody."

"I love Juan."

"Aha! I'd forgotten about Juan."

"I suggest you remember him so you can plan your trip. Once

he has gone, I'd be delighted to have you come back and spend a few days here."

Alejandra rose, went to her room, and brought me back a large envelope filled with other envelopes: letters which had been sent.

She said sweetly, "Read them. Maybe then you'll understand a little better."

I looked at her in surprise. Confiding in others and letting them pity her was not Alejandra's way. She guessed what I was thinking and said quickly, "I'm not expecting you to pity me, but maybe I'm expecting you to understand me. You think I'm one of that legion of half-crazy girls who run around coveting other women's husbands...."

"I have not said that...."

"No, you haven't said that or anything else. From the time you no longer dared take yourself seriously, you decided to take the entire world as a joke."

This time I was left speechless. She was right, a thousand times over.

"There is nothing worth taking seriously," I finally said, darkly.

"Not even Juan?"

I shrugged my shoulders.

"Read them," she repeated, and headed for the blazing sun of that January day.

I read them. I still have them in my hands. Tears are running down my cheeks as they do whenever I re-read your letters, yours, the letters I should never re-read. I promised you I wouldn't, I promised myself I wouldn't, and for at least five years I didn't; but one day three months ago, I couldn't control myself, and I read them. I am saying I read them, not *I re-read them*, so new and fresh they seemed. Because your love was immortal, it was eternally new and fresh. You loved me, you once loved me, maybe more than I did you...and so? Bob loved her, he once loved her. Why didn't she stay and fight to the finish? Foolish girl.

"Alejandra, Alejandra!" I shouted, looking out toward the

road, which shone yellow in the sunlight. But she's not there, she must have bicycled to the beach. Bob . . . his name is Bob, the man who wrote the same lies you did. One phrase, I think if I were to repeat just one of the phrases you wrote, in spite of the twelve years which have passed you would remember the words as if your pen were still putting them to paper: "because I know that I need you and you need me and that my presence in your life—which has been made up of astonishing revelations—can't come as a surprise." Bob is making the same statement, and Alejandra gravitated toward him, hypnotized, just as I toward you. I, you, what are we doing in all this? You had remained there in my past, blurry, until that November day when I made the crazy decision to betake myself to La Paloma. But it doesn't really matter. Bob is Alejandra's present. I can't leave her on her own. If I've lost you, why not be a mother in all seriousness instead of taking everything as a joke, as Alejandra says I do? Because I can't manage to love any of my three daughters as much as I loved you. I can't do it.

I rush to the garage and start the car. A terrible premonition, or rather memory, brings to mind the one solution Alejandra will be seeking. What's the use of living without Bob? If I were not her mother, that's what I would say to her: what's the use of living without Bob? You don't know how long and useless your days are going to be, how cold and empty your nights. How you'll laugh when the Belgian diplomat or your young admirers display their amorous intentions. I slap my forehead. I'm aware I've lost control. Alejandra can't drown, because she swims like a fish. Scientific studies have shown that in people who swim well the instinct for self-preservation wins out, and they return to shore. What's more, I have committed an unpardonable oversight in reading Bob's letters but not hers. I merely glanced at them, and the few lines I skimmed left me with the impression she was trying to be rational—to be rational about love! And she was making conditions, albeit slyly. I get out of the car, return to my room and pick up the letters I had spread out on my bed.

My poor Alejandra, so sensible, so rational, so conscientious in your duties—when I read your letters you seem born to be a schoolteacher in a quiet provincial city and grow old much esteemed by your neighbors and respected by your students. How could you, so in love, not have found another tone for your love letters, or at least a note, which would be in tune with Bob's passionate phrases? And on top of that, you allow yourself to give advice. How he should talk to his wife, how he should state the problem to his mother, to his son. You were not setting up an agenda for the monthly meeting of the campaign against hunger or illiteracy. You were afraid of yourself, of being too lyrical or too passionate. You wanted to appear strong, and that made you weak.

I do not wish to be unjust. My daughters have often reproached me for being hard on them and kind to the rest of humanity, even to complete idiots. But in this case I am being hard on myself. Her letters have the same defects mine did, those letters which helped me lose you. I re-read some of the letters. No, I am not mistaken: she waxes literary, there are references bordering on the pedantic. To top it all off, she boasts. She says she has countless invitations and doesn't even have time to sew on a button. She lunched with the ambassador and dined with the delegation from the Congo. A young man whom she showed around the city suggested they drive through Scotland together— dinners, cocktail parties, plays, lectures, caviar with one friend and spaghetti with others.... She feels she is Audrey Hepburn discovering Paris. And finally, as if she were a princess dreaming of escape from the ceremony of the royal house, she sighs, "...if only we could be together in a little white cottage in Majorca or Sicily and wake up beneath the dazzling sun, my head on your shoulder." Where did she get the idea there are little white cottages in Majorca or Sicily? I remember having lived there in the world's most luxurious hotels. I am also to blame. I poisoned her with literature of the last century. She thinks she and Bob might be able to repeat Chopin and George Sand's sojourn at the Charterhouse of Valdemosa, and she does not even know that it is the most inhospitable, and the windiest, spot on earth. Sometimes she is silly enough to say: "Ah, if I could send you a telegram instead of all these useless words!" Useless they are, but worse than that: they are ill- chosen. I must not tell her that. I must tell her only that, going by these letters, Bob adores her, and she must not lose him. Let her share him with his wife, with a monkey or a goat, but she must not lose him. Once she has lost him, as I did you, she will be a woman of no particular age who will not even cast a shadow on the rocks as she passes by. But I must not think about myself so much, nor about you. I must make what happened to me useful for my daughter.

All these letters are tangible evidence of Bob's security and Alejandra's insecurity. He does not mention his board of directors meetings or his business lunches. I've barely managed to figure out that he usually goes to Canada on his private plane. He speaks only of love. Because he is strong, he can do that. He is giving her a princely gift, and she is struggling in the net of a passion which weakens her. She thinks it best to keep that passion under control and not let Bob feel too secure.

I stop, thunderstruck: either I am suffering from an episode of hysterical mimesis or these letters...these letters are not theirs; they are ours. Why haven't I noticed before? Because of the names: she has my name; his is the same as yours. There is no tender word, no diminutive. Never did I say to you, as I had to other men, "my treasure, my beloved, my life, my love," nor did we call each other monkey, pussy cat, my dove, or anything else. The only words of love, the only ones which could encompass the immensity of the universe, the life force, the meaning of existence were our names, plain and simple. For me, your name encompassed all the love in the world. I am dizzy as I sort through the letters. In ours we'd say *usted*, addressing each other the formal Spanish way, except on unusual occasions. They do that too, but there are letters in English, and the difference between *usted* and *tú* doesn't come in there. I rummage through the letters, re-reading the same paragraph three times. They are all mixed together, and finally.... Good heavens, how slow I am. I understand: Alejandra has gone and brought our letters and theirs in the same packet. The most literary and theatrical are mine. I did that, I, my love! She did too. Bob is like you: strong and secure. Why was Alejandra determined to search for resemblances? Why did she go home, sort through my papers, and find the letters? And suddenly I know that, like me, she showed her love no mercy, she showed her good fortune no mercy, because her shoulders were not strong enough to support love and good fortune. Just then Alejandra came in and looked at me expressionless, not saying a word. I looked at her with the gaze of a madwoman, I fear. I didn't ask her "Why did you do it?" I screamed at her: "Why, why did you deceive him, you idiot? You loved him so much, so much...?" I was aware I was babbling and repeating all my words.

She nodded her head in agreement several times before replying, "What other defense is there?"

"Anything but that. It leads nowhere."

"I found out afterwards," she said with a shrug. "You find out everything afterwards."

Nothing could be done.

"And how did he find out?" I said.

Like an echo she replied, "How did he find out?"

"He found out nothing, nothing," I shouted. "What's more, it wasn't even deceit."

What does love have to do with the absurd gymnastics of two people who don't love each other? Sex...how that word is always tumbling out of their mouths! ...they think they discovered it, as if the rest of us had been produced in a test tube...sex does not exist. Love exists, desire, the madness of skin which does not live or breathe without the touch of the other's skin...which suffocates without that oxygen. Sex! Marvelous discovery—why not return to the brothel or the harem?

Silent, calm, Alejandra stood there in the doorway, still no expression on her face. That self-possession, that ability to remain silent is the great conquest of the women of the new generation. We were always talking, non-stop, with the grocer, the maid, our own friends, our grandmother's friends. We were a generation of females attacked by verbal diarrhea like a generation of males fallen prey to venereal disease. It is a question of era, style, upbringing, of I don't know what. I confine myself to setting down facts. In today's world, I never stop suffering unexpected shocks. On the streets of Leningrad I run into the daughter of a close friend. I have spooned cereal into her, I was present at her first communion and even remember giving her a medal to commemorate the event. I am surprised. I cry out and I rush toward her. Slowly, she turns around and says "How are things?" as if we were on a street in Buenos Aires and had seen each other the day before. Disconcerted, I think: What do you mean, *how are things?* The sensible thing is to ask, "What are you doing in Leningrad? How did you happen to come to Russia? Do you have any news of your mother? Your husband should be careful about taking that picture. Something happened to a friend of mine..." followed by a long, largely made-up story. All this kindness leaves her cold. She knows that we all travel, that it is as natural to run into each other here as it would be at Ricciardi's or another Buenos Aires department store. No doubt we'll run into each other in Paris next week, and we may even be on the same return flight. It is she who is right, but I can't get used to this attitude. My words are runaway horses rushing along, and I can't cut them off. Her husband comes up and says "How's it going?" Leningrad casts no spells. It would surprise us much more to run into each other at the La Plata Museum of Natural History than at the Hermitage. And young women are all like that.

Alejandra is in control of the situation. I decide to rise to her level and not ask from what cubbyhole she took the letters, nor how she had the nerve to take them, nor why she is combining two histories which have nothing in common but the words love and desolation. I get up, run a comb through my hair, which I pull back and fasten with a plastic barrette, and I point to the letters: "Put them in the envelope and try not to mix them up again. Yours on one side, ours on the other. I've already done enough work for one day."

Finally, there is a glimmer of surprise in her look. I have

managed to rise to the occasion and to the level of her generation. I exit. I shout from the living room, "Would you like a drink?"

"Whiskey," she answers back. It's the appropriate time. We are well-disciplined. We are not the sort of women who get drunk or drug themselves when they suffer disappointments.

After dinner we talked at length until nearly two in the morning—the start of the day when I began writing these pages.... The truth is that we came back late. We had dinner at Humberto's place. We went to the hotel and played baccarat since they don't have a roulette table; also, as usual I was the one who talked the most. I started out maternally, telling her she should stay, that I had telegraphed Juan to postpone his visit. She replied that, whatever the situation, her plans to go back to New York had been made. Her vacation was coming to an end; also, she wanted to see Bob. I tried to keep her here, but she was not to be appeased. She confessed she needed to see me, to see my failure (I definitely didn't like hearing that) in order to be sure she ought to live her love through to its conclusion, without pride, without listening to the advice of friends, who are always secretly malicious. We don't like hearing about someone else's good fortune. It's a fact. That makes for disenchantment with the world, I said. Why? Do rain, wind, and earthquakes lead to disenchantment with the world? No, they're facts; as such, one must accept them. Today, theoretically, one must accept everything. Her vocabulary isn't mine, either. She speaks of structures and schema, of states of conflict, and of accepting her responsibility, her age, her nationality, her sex, her skin color. Meanwhile, people are killing each other with these very words converted into the racket of machine-gun fire. But, between two long silences, these words ordain and expose fundamental truths. We used to talk non-stop. Our fathers used to contract venereal diseases.

January 17

This house must be haunted. I have reached the point of trembling with fright each time I hear a car stop or someone knock at my door. I wonder if this is a sign from divine providence that I should not try to isolate myself and should meekly spend the summer with all my friends close by. I don't know. The truth of the matter is that yesterday after lunch we were stretched out in our armchairs smoking, Alejandra and I. My cigarette was burning slowly between my fingers, hers quickly between her lips. Both of us were staring into the pine-cone filled fireplace as if in spell-bound contemplation of the red and green flames from a non-existent fire. Someone rang at the door. We didn't move. We didn't feel like receiving visitors. We had spent three days unsettled, without appetite, as if suffering from a bilious attack. In me were the old, unfortunate letters which I hadn't finished digesting; in her an inner conflict between pride and the ever stronger urge to return to Bob's arms. The bell rang again; then the bronze knocker struck the white wood; and finally, since I never lock it, the door sprang open, and I saw before me a smiling Rolando.

"Am I disturbing you?"

"No," I said, as I would have said yes.

"Juan," Alejandra said cheerfully, "it's good you came. I'm leaving tomorrow."

Rolando turned around to see if there was someone behind him and then, uncertainly, took in our obstinately stupid and inexpressive faces.

"It's fine, Juan. I'm not a little girl. I know Mama is expecting you. Come in, I'm pleased to meet you." First she called him *usted,* but then she switched to *tú.* She thinks the formal form of address old-fashioned and affected.

"I see I'm disturbing you," said Rolando. His voice was full of dignity and his expression murderous. "I am going to the hotel." He turned around and left, slamming the door.

Alejandra looked at me, disconcerted.

"What is going on? Is he crazy?"

"There are a lot of crazy people around here," I said, exhausted by so many days of futile explanations.

"In that case, you should bolt the door," Alejandra advised, getting up to do it herself.

She asked seriously, "Why are there so many crazies around here?"

"So many, no. By many, I mean a few. There is a home in the area."

"And you know this man?"

"Yes, he sells soap."

"Why soap?"

"Phew, you remind me of when you were a little girl, and you were always asking why. If I had told you he sold combs or hairpins, you would have asked me why he sells combs or hairpins and not soap."

"We had too much wine at lunch, didn't we?" inquired Alejandra, who smelled something fishy.

"No, it's not the wine. The problem is that his name is not Juan; it's Rolando."

"Do you know the crazies by name? I don't understand why it matters that his name is Rolando."

"What matters is that you called him Juan."

"And that offended him?"

"Look, we've spent more than enough days explaining things. It's quite simple. Figure it out on your own. I'm going to the hotel to right the wrong."

Alejandra exclaimed, "Aha! Now I get it!" And for the first time since her arrival she burst out laughing, bubbling over with uncontrollable, hearty laughter. I too burst out laughing, until we both got hiccups. Hiccups is a family ailment, the only one the various generations have encountered. Since we know all the remedies prescribed for this malady, we fill glasses with water, cover them with napkins and start taking small sips. For me this method never fails.

When we were through, she asked, "Are you going to the hotel?"

"I don't think it's worth bothering. He usually comes back on his own like a horse to the corral."

"Are you in love with him?"

"No."

"Is he in love with you?"

"No, he isn't."

"Then why the fit of jealousy?"

"I think that rather than jealousy it was annoyance at finding his place occupied by someone else."

"Is he in the habit of coming here often?"

"He spent a few days here. He said he would be coming for *Carnaval*, but he must have gotten his dates mixed up."

"And what does he come for if you don't love him, and he doesn't love you?"

"I didn't say that. We are quite fond of each other. Being in love is something different. Now, that will do. You know I've never been able to stand confiding in my daughters. The past few days I listened to you, that was my duty; I understood you, that was my right. You meddled in my past. I didn't want to lie to you. But I ask that you please leave my obscure present and rickety future alone."

"But what about Juan?"

"He does not exist. I simply wanted to be alone. That's why I came here. It didn't occur to me to call him Rolando nor give him the name of any of my friends since, in my opinion, none of these names sounds like that of a lover. The name of someone you love has a different sort of ring. It seems made up of letters from some other alphabet. That's why I invented Juan."

"In short, you wanted to get rid of me."

"You in particular, no. I need to be alone. I want to work. When I saw you suffering, I asked you to remain. You extended your stay, and I'm grateful. Now that will do. I detest long dialogues. They always end up turning sour."

Alejandra went to the door and unbolted it. She was no longer afraid of crazies. A gross error. Immediately the door sprang open as if by magic and before her terrified eyes Freddy appeared. This door was like a magician's top hat.

"Freddy," I exclaimed, laughing a hysterical laugh incomprehensible to him, "What in the world are you doing here?"

"And who is this?" Alejandra asked, worn out.

"This is Freddy."

By her look I saw she believed she had a nymphomaniac for a mother.

"He is a close friend of Iván and your sister," I said, already calmer.

"Ah! I seem to have come at a bad time."

"Not at all. I have to go out. Stay with Alejandra." And I went off without further explanation, banging the door. I was thinking of cancelling the rental agreement. Another week of living like this and I would go mad.

Now I had to face up to explaining things to Rolando. He will accept anything except the most simple explanation. His favorite sport is to seek out the line of reasoning opposed to that of the person addressing him. You, how this business of Juan and Rolando would have made you laugh. We would have laughed together. This sort of thing also used to amuse Santiago.

As I predicted, I had to face up to a long argument with Rolando, one of those harsh, dull arguments which leads nowhere, neither to bed nor to a breakup. Rolando believes in argument for argument's sake just as some believe in art for art's sake. In short, an exhausting day.

January 20

They've all gone: Alejandra to spend three days in Punta del Este, persuaded by Freddy; Rolando to Brazil by car, courageously, like someone who chooses the Foreign Legion. And I stayed put, alone; but I know that's not for long, since Freddy brought a letter from Nickie announcing her imminent arrival in Buenos Aires. She asked that I tell the super to open the apartment for her, because she counted on being at home there. Later she would be paying me a visit at La Paloma—to break up my solitude a little! Alejandra was happy to share the place with Nickie and

Facundo. She looked forward to seeing them. She was in a very good mood, giving me the impression Freddy's presence was making Bob's image fade a little.

To find one's destiny, there's nothing better than a change of place, I thought. The famous expression "If the mountain doesn't come to you, you go to the mountain" is a great metaphor. Why not emulate all those adored intruders and accept Marina's invitation to spend a weekend at her house in Punta del Este or go stay at my daughter's? I looked in the mirror. The truth is that if I don't head for civilization, I will end up transformed into wolf woman. My hair is uncombed, my face too brown—after a certain age sun must be taken in small doses—my nails unmanicured, my hands rough. These old blue pants, faded, look like a pair of Alejo's jeans. My shirt is masculine. I look like a lesbian. I am appalled. Get to work, I mutter while I remove my clothes, brush my hair, and get my best outfits from the closet. I want to see myself exactly as I will appear, none the worse for wear, at a Punta del Este cocktail party—just one, and then I shall come back here to go on living that great secret and romantic love they're all giving me credit for.

I look in the mirror. I am a magnificent parrot, a *oiseau des îles* you would have said, ready for export. As though my owner had shipped me again and again, his name is stamped on my left shoulder, my right nipple, both my thighs, where my back becomes rounded, and where my stomach curves in. I look perfect. Nobody can say I want to attract attention with my beige and white knits. I have turned almost invisible among the bright blues, the reds, the greens, the golden yellows, the white background. This riot of color is the indispensable camouflage which shows I have chosen to mimic my surroundings. The greater the proliferation of different colors my body displays the less attention I attract. All that's missing are a few gilt or silvery touches, some sequins, maybe long earrings which dangle and jangle, hitting my neck whenever I move—but I do have one or two pairs in the box on my night table. I put on the gaudiest ones and silver slippers too.

I had accounted for everything except that unpredictable

spirit which moves *La Barcaza.* I hear the door, and I rush into the living room. In front of me I see Nino, wide-eyed. "How awful," he mutters, adding, "Is that you?" What do you mean, is that me? Imbecile, uncouth savage, I think. It's me in all my finery, dressed for a party where you couldn't get in even as a waiter. It's me as I am in my daughter Dolores' fantasies, since she can't turn me into a bustling, silver-haired granny. But at least she'd rather see me taking my place among "my own kind" (according to her rather vague and dubious expression) than conversing with Luigi, Nino, or Humberto. "What's the problem, Nino?" I ask, worn out. "That's what I'd like to know. Why are you wearing a costume?"

"Because I'm going to a costume ball," I answer, pursuing his idea.

"Oh, good," he sighs, reassured. "Where, in Punta del Este?"

"Of course. And why did you come?" Suddenly I let fall on him all the annoyance caused by this endless invasion. "I arranged to stay in La Paloma so I could be alone, and I don't have a minute of solitude. People are coming and going as if this were a railway platform...."

"I came to bring you a letter. They gave it to me at the hotel, and I thought I would be doing you a favor."

"Oh, thank you. I'm sorry, but people are coming and going...."

"You already said that, but everybody complains that the same thing happens in weekend retreats around Buenos Aires and in Punta del Este."

"That's true, but here I notice it more. I think I'll have to return to Mar del Plata. At least there the huge mob of people allows us to vanish into almost complete solitude."

"Don't take the letter," he says, holding it out to me, not replying to my words, which he undoubtedly considers quite stupid.

I take the envelope and look at it. It is from Nickie, from Lisbon. She has already sailed. That's all I needed. I picture her pregnant. She must look like an olive with a toothpick stuck through it. She is quite delicate.

"Well," Nino says, not moving.

"I beg your pardon, it's from my daughter, but have a drink, if you like. I have good whiskey."

"Our little dump is full of whiskey, good and bad. What do I care about yours?"

Upset, I look at him. How dare he?

"What I care about is you. I can never be just with you.Either it's your daughters, your grandson, that friend who sniffs every mussel suspiciously, or your other daughter, or...."

"But we swim alone quite often...."

"People don't talk out in the sea," he says softly. "The sea isn't like land; it keeps people from lying, from saying foolish things, frivolous words."

"So much the better," I mutter.

I've collapsed into an armchair. Slowly I've taken off one earring, then the other. I'm aware my earlobes are hurting. My silver slippers are looking up at me like two hungry sharks. I look at them too. They are like two little frying pans. I have an urge to make myself two fried eggs.

Slowly, Nino tells me, "I paint too. Here we all paint."

"You paint? Why didn't you tell me before? I could give you some good advice. I am...."

"No thanks. Painting is already hard enough for me without adding the complication of advice from a successful painter."

"You don't like successful artists?"

"No, they are a sorry crew."

I jump up.

"I don't mean you, you had one or two successes by chance, but I think you don't care much about them. You're constantly searching for yourself. I notice it when I see you strolling on the beach or sitting among the rocks and watching the crabs scurry away or when you're swimming in that sexy way as if you were giving yourself to a man...."

Abruptly, he stops talking. And of course an awkward silence is established between us. In terror I think of a repetition of the scenario I lived through with Humberto. Even though this fellow is so young.... But it would be the same if I confessed to him—with irrefutable proof—that I am forty-nine and...but hasn't he seen me half naked on the beach? So then?

Ah, sunny, ardent twenty-five! Ah, thirty, sought after and sleepless! Ah, forty, aware and intense! Ah, time was so elastic once. It kept stretching out, and there was room for Santiago, and then you fit in (to fit in...as if the universe could fit into a sherbet glass). And now, these bursts of fatigue which shatter me like rounds from a poorly controlled machine gun. And now this figure—50—already standing out clearly on my horizon like a UFO, more real than the one Humberto saw, and even more eager to attack me, to crush me between its seemingly inoffensive jaws. Already I can't do too many things at the same time, and the day is coming when doing just one will seem miraculous. I will say proudly: yesterday I went to the theatre, today I have to pay a sympathy call, tomorrow my grandchildren are coming for lunch with their husbands and wives. Or maybe in the short interval which separates me from the finality of old age there will come to be no more theatres, nor visiting, nor grandchildren of the sort who lunch with their elders. Things will come to pass, unforeseen although not unforeseeable things. Other planets will invade us or we will conduct invasions against each other, and the more heavily populated the universe, the more man will be alone. The more science tries to approach God, the more abandoned will human beings feel in a world which has the skill to remove internal organs still throbbing with life from a body whose blood is still warm. Or maybe I won't end up as the little old woman of the fairy tales but will die earlier in an auto accident or plane crash, the way young people do, and my sudden death will rejuvenate me.

Nino is still standing right here, a demigod, barefoot, tanned, smiling.

"Pardon me, but this letter is urgent. We'll see each other on the beach tomorrow," I grow l.

He hesitates, he doesn't move. Does he want to strangle or assault me? To steal what? Wicker and canvas furniture, rustic tables, copper kitchenware? I signify something for him, something whose value can't be measured, but I don't know exactly what. Maybe my reputation as a painter and art critic. No doubt he wants me to paint the little shelter they have transformed into a restaurant or paint its walls and stamp my signature throughout. Or do a critique of his sketches for a Buenos Aires newspaper.

He comes closer. I think he's going to rape me, and a wave of pride rushes through my body clad in its multicolored come-hither garb. He takes me by the shoulders. He says in a deep, slow, firm, persuasive voice, which leaves no room for appeal: "Get away from this house as soon as possible...get away."

He releases me and goes running off. He has said, "Get away from this house," not away from the area. So I am right. There is something haunted here. Quickly, I change my clothes. I can't think things over calmly when I feel saddled up like a circus horse. I plant myself in front of the mirror. I look at my face and I look at my clothes. I address myself seriously: in coming to La Paloma, I swore I'd say, "Enough!" to frivolity, family obligations, and to love—which in any case almost always bids us goodbye before we resign ourselves to bidding it goodbye. I swore to finish my study of Manet and to paint for several hours every day. I have created almost nothing, except for my soups—three of lentils, two of garbanzos, and two of kidney beans—a pot of beef stew, and numerous fried eggs. All this put together does not justify a month of seclusion in a faraway, deserted expanse of sand. Of course, others have gotten in my way: Iván and Dolores, adorable Alejo from whom I must always keep my distance so as not to love him almost as much as I love myself, something against which I defend myself energetically, having been scalded by boiling water before; Freddy, the placid king of the commonplace; Alejandra, with her present emotional crisis which has revived memories of my past emotional crises; Rolando, with his imaginary rashes and the insomnia which surfaces after eleven hours of sleep; Nino;

Humberto; everyday life; and now this letter I hold in my hand. It has been mailed from a port. They're arriving! And to think there are people who take out newspaper ads in an attempt to find the family members left behind in Calabria or put on board a different boat in the course of a shipwreck! I too would take out ads, would move heaven and earth to reclaim these monsters who are devouring me. Sadism and masochism rule human relations; otherwise, they grow dull.

I put on faded blue pants, a blue T-shirt, take my box of paints and the canvas I fastened into its frame this morning and go down to the sea.

There, alone and unruffled, I open Nickie's letter. They arrive at the end of the week, that is, four days from now. I should tell Alejandra to leave them my room and sleep on the sofa in my studio. I should follow my impulse, take off for Punta del Este, talk to my daughters, and send a letter to Nickie inviting them to spend a few days in La Paloma. The hell with my forever-virgin canvas, my useless paintbrushes; after all, it's summer, and I'm on vacation. But there's the deep sea, and over there, as if beckoning me to plagiarize Van Dongen, the simple, oval shape of La Tuna Island, which I have been wanting to paint for a whole month. Why not say to hell with everybody and take my brushes, mix the colors on my palette, feel that slight tingling of fear and desire which comes over my skin whenever I begin a new work?

But it is so hard for a woman on her own to make heroic decisions. The beaten path confers a measure of peace and relieves one of responsibility. I paint a while, as if to stay on good terms with my calling before giving in to convention. I pack a bag with the clothes which so terrified Nino, plus some pants and casual blouses, my creams, my brushes and pencils for lips, eyebrows and lashes—that useless arsenal for a battle already lost. I climb in the car and right away feel the pleasure of the road, the vertigo of speed, that infinite happiness brought about by travelling the highways and byways of the world. Why have I deprived myself of this pleasure for a month? Only once did I go as far as Rocha and

I didn't dare continue on to San Carlos as suggested by the Belgian diplomat's wife in her enthusiasm for the local leathercraft. I was afraid to go on ahead and did not want to go to Punta again, to the social life, to the temptation—arduous and bland at the same time—of following the crowd.

The road is intoxicating me. I think of nothing but the marvelous momentum rushing me along this cheery, undulating road between two lines of trees, in this land made for happiness, laziness, and generosity.

January 23

In Punta del Este I didn't find time to record any of my impressions, of course. Things didn't happen exactly the way I had supposed they would. Dolores and Iván greeted me with surprise. I was moved only by Alejo's little face, which glowed as he threw himself silently and eloquently into my arms. The guest room was being occupied by Alejandra, but Iván reminded me I had an unconditional invitation from his mother: "any day, any time, for as long as you wish," and we headed for her house. Marina greeted me with a welcoming smile which faded as soon as she learned I planned to stay there. Of course she did have a room free, but Jacques is such a recluse. Visitors bother him. It must be remembered he is not a wild creature of the pampas like us but a man suffering from war trauma, and thus he has every right. He had almost been imprisoned in a concentration camp, his father had narrowly escaped being shot, his three brothers had crossed the Alps on foot, then the maquis country of southern France; after that, by the skin of their teeth they had crossed the frontier into Spain, finally landing in Algeria to join the free forces. Except they arrived a little late, the day after the armistice. But these things leave their mark on a man. I didn't quite understand what connection could be established between my weekend in his house and concentration camps, firing squads, electrified border fences, and free forces, but I listened as I would at mass, humble, humiliated, obliging, submissive, and filled with remorse over disturbing the lives of persons whose destiny was far superior to ours. In spite of everything, she would put me up that night. It was easier and more comfortable to go to a hotel, but I was already so beaten down I didn't know how I could escape. I settled into a lovely sun-filled bedroom furnished in luxurious good taste. I bathed and got ready to attend the evening's four cocktail parties. Since it was Tuesday, there was not too heavy a schedule.

I attended the cocktail parties. They greeted me with open arms, with that artful, mystifying hospitality which springs up in Argentineans as soon as they move abroad even if it's just across the border. No one stared at me with Nino's horrified look. I was a parrot among other parrots, who were for the most part more elegant and showy than I. A few women ventured a compliment. With suspicious looks they noticed my dress, a designer creation just as theirs were. I suppose they believed mine apocryphal. They didn't like it much; clearly, it's because I lack personality. It would have impressed them more to see me arrive in a sweater and faded pants, but it is not in my power to have personality in this kind of dispute. I meekly accept the directives of other women with the thought that no one can fight on all fronts. On other fronts, I engage in battles which I care about deeply. I win and lose like everyone else. To fight against an embroidered dress or a blouse in all colors of the rainbow is beyond my strength. Nevertheless, I do note that I'm disappointing the winners. They don't picture me like this, and I don't please them like this. They want me worthy of my paintings, my art criticism, and my prize at the Venice Biennale. They don't want us to be equals. We are not. Among themselves, they will praise any old outfit, and they don't believe it appropriate to praise mine. My position in society is rather uncomfortable. While the magazines talk of my leopard coat "just like Liz Taylor's" and my luxury apartment, "where soft carpeting muffles entering footsteps" (as if these were irrefutable arguments for rejecting my art), my friends with other leopard coats, other carpets, declare me a genius but pretend not to see I am decked out in the latest model of the same uniform they are wearing. They asked if I had done much work in La Paloma. What an ideal place! It's a dream, that's the truth, what peace. That's how Europeans spend the summer, not all piled on top of each other the way we are. This isn't a rest. I'm going to Buenos Aires to rest. Each phrase came out in its predictable form, like chocolate bars out of a vending machine. It was a question of putting the coin in the right slot, and all of us would say what we were supposed to say. I ended up wondering whether a giant ventriloquist was making us speak against our will.

We weren't very brilliant or very original; but were we brilliant and original at Humberto's or Luigi's? We had human warmth, a desire to like each other, to make life enjoyable, to flee the shadows of the past, present, and future.

The following day Jacques asked with his sweetest smile if I had taken care of lubricating the car and checking the oil since I would no doubt be leaving that very afternoon. I told him everything was in order and that my first activity would be lunch with my daughters because we had important matters to talk over. Then Marina began showing an interest. What was it about? Had I heard from Papa? Was he still living with that adventuress? But he never lived with any adventuress, I answered, indignant. She is quite a respectable woman and is sacrificing herself for a man who has very little to give her. What do you mean, very little? What about the apartment in Portofino? Even though men are such idiots, I would hope he's put it in your name! Why are you going to let them dispossess you and dispossess your daughters? The word dispossess never fails to amuse. If that apartment fell into my possession, my daughters could be sure they wouldn't see even the doorknobs. I was determined to spend any such inheritance on a world tour. But I thought it fair that the place be left to his companion of the past twelve years, the woman tending his imaginary bouts of hepatitis, his imaginary attacks of cirrhosis, his imaginary cancers, and his very real unpleasant disposition. But Marina didn't understand it that way. Her son was married to Dolores, and it's fine that there's no dowry in Argentina, but there is inheritance, isn't there? We aren't behind the Iron Curtain. You yourself ought to think about putting your apartment in your daughters' names; after all, that wouldn't change anything. You could enjoy it as long as you're alive and your art gallery too. It's worth a lot today, don't you know? I didn't know whether to get mad or burst out laughing. Jacques had judiciously left the scene. I chose to avoid the subject and claimed I was running late. I said we could talk all this over another time. Maybe tonight at dinner, ventured Marina, not remembering her hints: that night her son would no doubt be arriving with a friend. My presence couldn't really be called a nuisance, but it was creating complications in the sleeping arrangements. I did not reply. I climbed in the car and said goodbye with a hearty wave. My bag was packed, and I planned to pick it up while they were at their club, one of those inevitable clubs which Argentineans—the most insecure creatures on earth—strew in their path, burning up lawns and flowers like Attila the Hun just so they will know exactly who each of them is and who is across from them. And in this sweet earthly paradise, with a shore more unspoiled than Argentina's, they strove to repeat the mistaken behavior which had kept the vacationers on our beaches separated by means of barbed wire.

Alejandra and Dolores appeared to have been briefed by Marina. They recounted how Nickie had seen Papa. He had really gone downhill and looked much older than four years ago. Come on now! If he looked younger, that would be odd! I should go visit him and see for myself whether this woman wasn't taking everything. Already impatient, I said: But what in the world would you have her take, if he only has his pension and the amount he ended up with after selling his house in Olivos? And that doesn't seem like much to you? You're not thinking of us or of your grandchildren. There's no reason he should spend the entire pension. He could keep a little each month. At his age, watching television all the time, it would be enough. He could buy dollars, invest them in one of those funds.... I was exasperated. Leave him in peace, I shouted. He's a charming old man who does not ask anything of you, is not inconveniencing anyone, and is living the way he wants to. I haven't come to talk about him but to give you the house key, which you forgot, Alejandra. Set yourself up in the studio. Tell Nickie and Facundo to come but to please let me know.... Apparently another forbidden phrase! That's the limit, to have to let your mother know you're coming to her house! Don't pull this nonsense about mothers, I said finally, losing my temper: I want you to let me know. I have the same rights you do. I couldn't come to your house unexpectedly in spite of the invitation, because you had no room. Alejandra prefers to live in New York without giving a damn about whether I'm alone or have companionship. Nickie went down the aisle four months pregnant...and, I've said enough! In the ensuing silence I leaped into the precipice once again: I am a woman on my own, I live with whomever I please, and if there's no room in my house you'll go off to a hotel. Don't demand so much maternal love when you never think about filial love. Duties for me, pleasures for you—no, my dears. Neither Papa nor I are ready for sackcloth and ashes and a diet of macaroni twice a day just so you can have sports cars. Get that straight once and for all. I've said enough.

As the morning went on, we tried to soothe spirits but not much came of it. I merely insisted she turn over the double bed to Nickie, remember to turn off the gas, not leave lights on unnecessarily, and inform the super of their presence so he wouldn't think thieves had broken in.

I arrived back at night, so exasperated that I went out in the warm, humid air and walked toward the lighthouse to calm myself. The trip in the car had already soothed me a little. I went to Humberto's place, late. It was crowded. I met a charming woman, the first woman I've made friends with since arriving in La Paloma. Her name is Diana. She is a writer and photographer, the first time I've come across the two professions together. The artists and writers I know can't take even a childish photo and they don't appreciate music. We are very limited people. That's not a criticism. I believe in being limited in order to devote oneself to a single branch of art. The giants, Leonardo and Michelangelo, are the exception: the rest of us, once we become familiar with one artistic idiom, only succeed in expressing ourselves in that particular idiom. To attempt more turns us into dilettantes. She invited me to dinner tonight. Her house is extremely ugly, and I made the observation that there were others she could have rented. She said she hadn't taken a good look at the house even though she's been in it a week. To her, it could just as well be a tent. I understood.

January 25

Last night Diana related her history, an ominous destiny filled with curses. She is recounting it in her memoirs. She gave me some pages to read and I'm copying them. I don't think any of it is true. Theoretically, novelists have imagination. If that's not so, then they're living ten or fifteen lives instead of just one like the rest of us. Listening to her and reading her work makes my problems seem everyday, minor, and just like everyone else's. Her problems seem different. Maybe I'm wrong. I've copied a few pages:

DIANA'S TALE

"One of my ancestors (I know not for certain if he was my great-or my great-great grandfather) dedicated himself to a trade, now outlawed, which brought riches to many a well-born gentleman at the dawn of the eighteenth century. I refer to trafficking in black slaves. Faded documents from that era show he used to transport blacks from Cabo Verde Island, where he had settled, to the shores of Brazil, where he would sell them for a good price. The trade prospered since the climate suited the slaves, who flourished, grew stout and strong, and delighted their new owners. Coming back on yet another voyage, my ancestor would not encounter frowning faces, but on the contrary welcoming smiles, backslapping, and congratulations on a keen eye for choosing slaves. In his shipboard diary he tells hair-raising stories hardly suitable for repeating in the twentieth century. He speaks of a smallpox epidemic during which all the slaves stayed shut up in the hold, dead and living together, some in a state of putrefaction; but not a single sailor wished to venture through that doorway. What a fortunate man my grandfather would have been in the era of vaccinations! His blacks, vaccinated like cattle, would not have contracted so many mortal pestilences. However, no matter how much he might stuff his ears with cotton (wax plugs were not as yet invented) and cover his head with a pillow, the shrieking would come through the gleaming wood walls of his cabin as forcefully as the roar of a storm. He could hear the cries of the dying black men and of the black women giving birth while ripping their ankles open to the bone because they could not spread apart their legs, fastened with fetters and chains. 'Cursed, cursed creature!' was the expression which reached him the most distinctly despite his attempts to drown it out with rum. Twenty years of uninterrupted curses have to undermine the morale of any man. At forty-two my great-grandfather was old and wan, sad-eyed, balding, and rather stooped."

"Old age does not necessarily mean purity, especially in a slave trader. To be an honorable old man one must have been a passionate, idealistic young one. A little roguish behavior is insignificant, but not trafficking in human beings. Don Alfonso, for such was his name, at times wondered how those curses would manifest themselves. In his heart he believed in them as would any Christian sprinkled with baptismal water. He was of course a lecher, a womanizer. He was wont to satisfy his libidinous urges while having whipped before his eyes the most beautiful of the female slaves and, on occasion, adolescent male slaves. In obscene pages, he tells what took place between him and the women. What took place with the beardless youths or what they suggested to him he does not mention. One day, my grandfather sent away his sailors and their scourges as they prepared to whip a fourteen-year-old girl whose buttocks were as round as cherries. He possessed her exactly as they had presented her to him, not even bothering to untie her. Then he set her up in a cabin and kept her there for his personal solace."

"It was noon on a February day when the hot beauty of Río de Janeiro Bay took them into its bosom, as if into a blazing bonfire. Don Alfonso locked his concubine in the cabin, went to visit his usual customers, got drunk in the bars where he was a loyal and sought-after patron, and returned to the ship, his business finished. The following day he delivered the merchandise and charged the prices agreed upon, although he did surprise his customers a little when he appeared more flexible than usual and did not haggle unduly over reducing brawny slaves who looked like ebony statues."

"Don Alfonso was in a hurry. He returned to his vessel, took Consolación—such was the name he had given the barely pubescent black girl—and carried her off to Ouro Preto. Brazil's first capital received them on its narrow cobblestone streets, under its French tile roofs, among its houses with their thick whitewashed walls which the blazing sun of the Brazilian summer never scorches. Consolación was left in the care of an old nursemaid who rounded out her meager monthly income playing procuress. A despairing Don Alfonso set out once more to resume his slave trafficking. He had calculated he would be back for the birth of the child. And so he was, since the old scoundrel never made a mistake in any calculation, not even the least certain. They had six or eight children. I do not know the exact number. I know only that Don Alfonso, at the risk of earning less money, would always remain in Ouro Preto from the birth of one child until the conception of the next. He did not like leaving his paternity to chance."

"Here there are some blanks in the history. I believe there were some children born dead, and others carried off by plague. According to Don Alfonso's documents, one of them turned out to be a sculptor; unfortunately, leprosy ate away his hands, but he went on sculpting with hooks fastened to his stumps, until he had completed twelve giant apostles. I wonder if that is the truth. I wonder if Alejandinho is the son of the heartless slave trader and the young black woman conquered by force. With family documents, one guess is as good as another; in general, when they fall into our hands they are in flagrant contradiction with the stories we heard as children from our mothers and our nurses, stories which aren't consistent with each other either, by the way."

"One day the storm was unleashed: the fifteen-year-old daughter, slender, tall, delicate, an almost white mulatto, fell madly in love with a black man as handsome as she. The marriage had been agreed upon in Don Alfonso's absence, and it did not occur to Consolación he might raise objections. He had never paid much attention to his children; he merely provided what was necessary for feeding them and sheltering them under a poetic roof of mildewed tiles. He would pat them on the head as he passed by. When told the oldest was sculpting in stone, he would shrug and exclaim, 'These mulattos are all lazy creatures.' Then he would shut himself away with his shadow, that black flesh which had intoxicated him the first time the whip had cracked and was now satisfying those autumnal desires, as difficult to satisfy as those of adolescents, who feel cheated at the simplicity of the sexual act compared to the unbridled sensuality of their solitary pleasures. Consolación merited her name. Only she could still bring pleasure to this ragbag stuffed with money and remorse."

"When Don Alfonso learned Angustias wished to marry a black man, the house shook from top to bottom as if struck by an earthquake. He was a man of quick decisions. Without further concern for his black woman, who had aged and grown heavy, he took his favorite daughter and went off without saying where. It seems that Angustias, sobbing, clung to her mother, who begged him not to snatch away her beloved child. Don Alfonso tied Angustias to the bannister, took Consolación by the arm and led her off to the bedchamber. As he left, three or four hours later, he said: 'Now I've made you another child. You can do without this one.' Consolación dared not protest. She was accustomed to submission. Besides, blacks were not liked in Ouro Preto, where people boasted of preventing their taking over, and wealthy owners castrated their slaves along with their cattle."

"Everyone thought Don Alfonso would carry his daughter off

to Europe, but taking her to Buenos Aires seemed much shorter to him. Moreover, it was easier to find her a husband here. There were throngs of blue-eyed, blonde adventurers who could give him lily-white grandchildren. Truthfully, such miasmas arise from his documents that it is not slander when I venture to declare he felt for Angustias something more than deep paternal love. For that old beast, incest was probably a venial sin."

The manuscript Diana gave me ended here. I was left shaken and full of curiosity. But I usually do my reading at night, and it was already 3 a.m., so I couldn't run and ask her how all this had ended. I felt I was back in the era of the magazine serial. One had to wait for the next issue. I had lascivious dreams that night, and I woke up nervous and exhausted. Getting out of bed was an effort. I drank a glass of milk and lay down again, on my back, hands behind my head, listless and disoriented. I thought of you, faraway and unattainable, of my stubborn chastity, of Humberto's pitiful efforts, and I believe I even envied Consolación.

Before going to the beach, I stopped by Diana's house to leave the manuscript. I entrusted it to María, who works there too and who informed me her other employer was at Bahía Chica.

And, indeed, I found her conscientiously taking in the sun. She was covered with expensive creams, filters, and moisturizers which protect from overexposure to solar rays. It surprised me there could be a drop of black blood in this blonde white woman whose skin blistered if at all neglected. I stretched out next to her and asked if her tale contained some element of truth.

"But it's the unadulterated truth," she exclaimed.

"And why are you so white? You turn red as soon as the sky is cloudless."

"Ah, that's my Jewish blood," she said indifferently.

I am not racist, or I don't think I am. I am surrounded by people who are not or who pretend they are not, but this urge to have Jewish blood in addition to black blood is not common in my circle.

"Do you really have Jewish blood or are you suffering from

an unusual mania and wish all the bloods of the world ran through your veins? Why not Arab, why not Asian?"

"Asian is not likely," she said, "but Arab is. I have studied my family tree extensively. What happens is that here in our America people have never studied theirs. To gain your respect, it would be enough to tell you I am a descendant of the Marquis Don Alfonso de Narvajas Salazar y Vargas. But if I told you the true story of said marquis and his black concubine you would consider me somewhat nutty."

"Maybe," I said. "But you did leave me intrigued. What happened with Angustias?"

"She married a Dutch gem dealer. It's a shame he didn't leave me some diamonds to pay for all these nasty creams I'm obliged to use because of his blood, which in me is more dominant than any other."

"And they were happy?"

"Happy?" screeched Diana, as if I had just told her they had been murderers. "Happy? But then you didn't understand any of it! How can they be happy, these descendants of the hundreds of blacks who cursed them from their stinking holds, blacks with ulcerated flesh, mangled hands, and their women whipped and possessed before their very eyes. Don't you believe in anything? Don't you believe in God?"

"I suppose so," I muttered.

"Then don't talk to me about happiness. Down to the fourth generation our family has been cursed. The black man they separated from Angustias snatched out his eyes, pulled out his teeth and nails so he wouldn't be sold as a slave to procreate other slaves or work for his tormentors. Every day Alejandinho would take him cornmeal porridge Consolación had prepared. I think he finally hanged himself from a tree. He did the right thing."

We were silent.

"Don Alfonso," Diana went on slowly telling her story, "had given his daughter a magnificent dowry, but he had forced his son-in-law to accept a condition: he would hand over the money little by little as children were born. If they were blonde and blue eyed, the reward was greater. And so Angustias found herself sentenced to procreate as her mother had, according to the will of her lords and masters. She produced eight blonde, blue-eyed children, and one black as black could be. The Dutchman, not knowing of his wife's heritage, was horrified. He brought the child to her, killed it before her very eyes, and disfigured her permanently by throwing muriatic acid in her face. He didn't kill her, because he needed her to raise his other children. I am descended from one of them."

Diana turned over on her right side and covered her face with a straw hat.

"And what about the other children?"

"At the age of sixteen the oldest was kidnapped by pirates. They kept him handcuffed in the hold of their ship. Although they had collected the ransom, they let him rot as my grandfather's slaves had rotted in their dungeons. The second child, a girl, was raped by an exhibitionist. While playing hide-and-seek in the park suddenly there appeared before her what seemed to be a monster but was merely a male with an erection. She stood there terrified, and the sadist raped her, leaving her pregnant. She didn't dare tell her mother, to say nothing of her father, whom she feared as if he were a god. Don Alfonso also commanded her respect. The poor girl believed herself to be a member of a normal, moral, well-established family. Everybody believes that and almost nobody is. When they found out, it was too late for an abortion. They shut her away on a ranch and married her to a farmhand. The third child lost his mind at the age of eighteen, outfitted himself in a suit of armor displayed in the drawing room, then set out for the Crusades...."

"Hi, there. Who are you gossiping about now? I'll bet it's some of your friends in Punta del Este."

We returned from the other world only to see before us the Belgian Embassy official's wife, as jolly as usual. We noticed that a few feet away her children were dissecting a baby shark.

Nino approached, walking with his rhythmical sea gait. Nino! the thought suddenly came to me. Why not? My imagination was mixing almost indissolubly images of the black men described by Diana and the very real figure of this bronzed young man. I seemed to catch a look of complicity between him and Diana. Of course! Why hadn't I thought of that before? He was the ideal man for a woman from such a lascivious and unprejudiced family. I felt an unrestrainable urge to tell them I was not just a nice bourgeois lady who painted portraits to earn a few pesos, that Alejandra was carrying on with a married man, that my father was a dirty old man living with a charming woman in Portofino. . . . But it wasn't the same. We remembered to send each other Christmas cards and to exchange birthday gifts. We believed we were more or less familiar with the unexciting origin of our red blood, which had taken on a tinge of blue thanks to academies of science, boards of directors of major companies, governing bodies of exclusive clubs. And Santiago died without abandoning ship, all alone, and no one has ever learned if he felt fear, if he fired a shot before going under, or if he tried to swim, tried to emerge from that enormous apocalyptic mouth which opens up in the sea, devouring conquered ships and their valiant captains.

January 26

Diana entrusted me with more pages from her memoirs. I feel cheerful. When I read them, I forget everything. The menacing danger represented by my daughters, with their problems and their untimely visits, turns into child's play compared to these adventures. It's the first time in my life I've met anyone who tells such tales or who is descended from buccaneers. Although what I'm saying is completely stupid. It wouldn't be logical for pirates and slave traders not to have left any trace of their stay on earth nor any descendants. I seem to believe they existed only so that we today could make technicolor films.

DIANA'S TALE CONTINUED

"Angustias fourth child, a son, was blessed with an angelic

beauty comparable only to that of the sister who came after him and was eleven months younger. Gazing at those two porcelain creatures consoled Angustias for the state of repulsive ugliness which forced her to keep her face veiled like women in seraglios and rather suited her status as a semi-slave. Besides being lovely, these two children were affectionate. Instinctively, they loved their mother more than their father, and poetic intuition told them that the bruised, burned, purple face and the mouth without lips were not simply the result of an accident."

"These two youngsters could not live without one another. Intuitively, when apart, each sibling could tell exactly what was going on with the other. I know they disappeared together from the family circle at the age of seventeen, and no one in my family ever spoke of them again. Yet, whenever I'm raiding attics and lofts, crates and dilapidated trunks, I come across photographs of them, locks of light blonde hair, clothes and toys which had been theirs. My grandmother had pasted into a notebook newspaper clippings about the family. A double suicide is mentioned there—a brother and sister, aged thirty. The names and photographs left no room for doubt. What happened between them over those thirteen years? No one ever found out. The rest lived what appeared to be normal lives, although on reaching the age at which my grandfather had sailed with his first cargo of blacks some catastrophe would befall them. They died young, ruined victims of crime or suicide. The lucky ones enjoyed the grace granted some offenders: the gallows instead of the stake; that is, they would die in accidents."

"My siblings and I grew up watchful and timid. We would often get together secretly to seek a way of escaping the curse. Among the five of us we had reconstructed the family history without worrying too much about some insurmountable gaps. Our mother had committed suicide two days after the birth of the last of us, a creature of indeterminate sex, with webbed extremities instead of human hands and feet. The poor monster lived barely a week but it was too late to bring Mama back to life."

"One day...."

Here the second part of the tale ended. Since I knew from Diana that this was the true history of her family and not the work of her imagination, I spent a sleepless night trying to think whether any of my ancestors might have merited a similar curse.

The following afternoon I went to visit Diana. Contrary to her custom, she was not alone. Next to her sat an elderly woman, knitting. Her white hair with its blue tints had been carefully styled. Her eyes were bright, her smile gracious.

Diana said by way of introduction, "This is the oldest of my cousins."

I shuddered at the thought that this woman came from the stock which had been making chills run up and down my spine. But there was nothing out of the ordinary in the atmosphere. Diana served tea. Her cousin told me she was in Uruguay because her best friend had just been run over by a car. She had been with her grandchildren, seven-year-old twins, who had also died in the accident.

"How horrible!" I cried out, now feeling subconscious dread over striking up a friendship with this ominous family. "How I sympathize with you...please accept my condolences. You must be quite distressed."

She gave me a surprised look. "Not me," she said. "I am alive and in this charming spot."

"Ah, well...but, after all, to see people dear to you crushed under the wheels of a car."

"My girl," she said in a slightly pompous tone, "you don't know human nature very well. There's nothing like somebody else's catastrophe to make us enjoy our own advantages more. To tell you the truth, my friend's life used to interfere with mine. Very few women obtained the posts and honors she did, and that was always a thorn in my side."

"Two lumps?" Diana asked, her expression unchanged.

"No, no, saccharine," I stammered.

"In the end, almost every life is a failure. The one that looks like a success, even just on the surface, rubs us the wrong way. Quite often I tried to stay away from her so I wouldn't carry around that burden of envy which is so uncomfortable. It's like a corset that's too small, with stays sticking out." She laughed at her witticism. "But it was awkward. We would meet here and there. I would feel obliged to congratulate her. The truth is, her death is a great relief...a great relief," she repeated with a sigh of satisfaction.

I thought she was a harmless lunatic and that Diana hadn't been able to warn me because of my untimely arrival. But Diana didn't give that impression at all. I sought her gaze, I made faces, and she looked surprised.

"Will you be spending many days in La Paloma?" I asked Cousin Engracia.

"No, two or three days. Now I'll be more content anywhere in the world. The truth is, I still have more than enough people on my horizon. Diana, for example. Luckily, I'm richer than she is, and that allows me a certain superiority. What's more, her childhood was so sad and mine so happy that the two compensate for each other, don't you think?"

I burst out laughing, believing she had made a joke. Diana smiled faintly.

"Don't laugh; Engracia is speaking in all seriousness. It's just that she says things other people keep to themselves. When I won the Galatea Prize, she called and said, 'What an unpleasant morning I've had. So many other people could have won this prize, and you got it merely to make me spend a miserable day. The one consolation is knowing everyone will say it's unfair, that you had an in with the jury, that you were somebody's lover, or that all the other entries were so bad they settled on yours.'"

"But that's awful," I said, sincerely angry.

"It isn't very nice," Engracia said, "but most of her friends felt the same way and kept quiet about it. I at least didn't lie. Besides, such truths are useful for helping artists keep their feet on the ground. So often, you're living on the moon!"

"And you're a descendant of one of Diana's aunts or uncles?"

"Yes, Nieves and Arnoldo."

"Yes, but which one is related to Diana?"

"Both of them. They went off together. Don't you know the story?"

I shuddered. I was beginning to admit that outside of my usual circles more interesting people were to be found, but they were also more fearsome.

During the days this woman with the pleasant, charming manners stayed in La Paloma, I heard her say things which may not be at all extraordinary, but which nobody up to then had come out with in my hearing.

Sunday morning she devoutly attended mass, and as she put her coins in the plate, she whispered, "For father to spend in the bar." Then she paid to have masses said for the soul of her dead friend.

"I don't understand," I said, "why you are having masses said if you hated her."

"But where do you get such horrible ideas, child? I adored her. It was just having her around that was unbearable. But now that she's dead, how can she trouble me? Come on, don't play the little girl. These are everyday feelings. I've discussed them often with my brother, who is a priest and hears many confessions."

Later, as we were heading for the beach she talked to me about myself: "Do you have children?"

"Yes, I have three daughters...."

"Oh, my goodness! What bad luck! And you such a charming woman!"

"But it's not bad luck at all. I have wonderful daughters. One of them...."

"I know, I know, but don't forget they belong to a generation of iconoclasts and parricides. They are the only people in the world who one way or another would like to see you dead, except of course for some very close friend whom you overshadow...but children...they are a danger!"

My feelings of fascination and repulsion were struggling with each other. A sort of spell emanated from this tiny woman on whose face the same smile always hovered and who spoke of the most sacred subjects with the cruelty of a seasoned philosopher or a condemned poet. The unusual circumstance that she was the daughter or granddaughter of an incestuous union (something I half believed) led me to be kind. How much truth and how much falsehood was there in this somber history which the entire family—at least the members I'm acquainted with—boasted of with that pride which comes of being an exception?

I left Engracia at the house and headed for the beach with Diana. Once there, my body stretched out in the sun and my face protected by the umbrella, I told her the manuscript had distracted me from all my personal problems but I was still wondering what had happened to the other children and which one she had descended from.

"I will tell you, but I have still not come to my mother's story; actually, at the moment I am summing it up with the help of some old papers."

"But you at least seem to have been spared the fateful curse uttered by the blacks who were crowded into the holds of the ancestral vessels."

"No," she said, "I have been spared nothing."

"Aha."

"I will go on telling you my life story...as long as it interests you, obviously."

"Of course, that's why I came to La Paloma."

She gave me a strange look. "I don't see the relationship...."

"Oh, forgive me. I came here hoping to meet people who were different. Until you came, I could only say once again that people are the same everywhere. A faded sweater doesn't necessarily create a more striking personality than a fancy beaded dress. Your showing up has saved me from ending my vacation disillusioned."

She shook her head thoughtfully. "I think you're oversimplifying. There are many people with interesting histories and pirate ancestors, but they keep quiet about it. In my daily life, I'm not much different from anybody else. Except things happen to me that are different. I have always lived balancing on a rocky ledge. But nobody notices."

"And your cousin?"

"Her case is different."

"Why does she hate young people?"

"She doesn't hate them, but she fears them. Because of her fear she dresses like an older woman, leaves her hair gray, won't come to the beach. She does not want to compete with them in any sphere. She says that's the only way they leave her in peace. The result is a darling little old lady who does not contend for her place with anyone, not even on this vast beach. She is calm, egotistical, and inexorable. She claims these are three states essential for living in peace, for not creating bad blood, for avoiding a heart attack, and for living to a ripe old age. She is barely sixty and acts ten or fifteen years older. If it weren't for her smooth complexion and caustic words you probably would have thought her much older."

"That's true. And what do the young people in the family think of her?"

Her look grew somber: "There are no young people in my family. We all swear that the curse will end with us."

"But they've all taken it seriously?" I asked, overwhelmed. "I thought that much of it was fiction."

Diana gave me a withering look and jumped to her feet: "I'm going in the water," she said without answering my question.

I have spent three or four days obsessed with my new friends. I have hardly seen anyone else. Today I intend to shake off this evil enchantment and dine at The Magic Seashell.

February 1

Last night Humberto greeted me with a show of happiness. It pleased me that my absence had been noticed. However, when I said goodbye around 1 a.m., Humberto accompanied me to the door, saying in a serious tone, "I have to talk to you."

"To me? About what?"

We started walking toward my car. I saw that initiating this conversation was an effort for him. He hemmed and hawed. He seemed uncomfortable and didn't know whether to speak up or keep quiet. Life has taught me it's always better to keep quiet since people don't want to hear anything at all that might interfere with their plans or force them to face problems which could be put off until later. But Humberto seemed to feel the bad news he had to convey was extremely important. For a moment I thought something had happened to one of my daughters and that he had been given the task of breaking it to me as gently as possible.

"Speak up. I don't understand any of your gibberish. What is going on? What is this danger you're talking about? Why are you telling me to be cautious?"

"It's nothing momentous. Don't be alarmed. But you are not used to places like this. I've lived here fifteen years, and I've seen every kind of human fauna pass by. You aren't part of a closed group where everybody knows your great-grandparents or is somehow related to you. Here you come upon people of every description. For several days you have abandoned us for those women who live in that horrible house next to Solari Beach..."

"Aha, that's all it is! I know a great deal more about them than any of you do. Diana is an extraordinary woman, a historian. Her cousin is quite amusing. It's as if she stepped out of an old play you might have heard of, called *Arsenic and Old Lace*. She could commit murder with a glass of chilled *horchata* or any other tasty, healthful beverage, for that matter. These two have a fantastic background. To be frank, because of them I feel justified for having come and buried myself here instead of strutting around Punta del Este like everyone else."

"Like everyone else! What an idiotic statement!"

"How rude you are!"

He shrugged his shoulders.

"Let's stop skirting around the margins and get right into the thick of the text," I said sarcastically.

"It's such a pleasure to converse with intellectuals," commented Humberto in the same tone. "What is not in the margin but in the text is that your friends are out-and-out lesbians."

I let out a shriek.

A triumphant Humberto went on hurling his barbs: "Have they ever had husbands? Do they have children? Do you ever see them looking at men? Come on, don't play naïve. The bad thing is that this is compromising you, since nobody here knows of any lover of yours...."

"What, no one knows of any lover?" I asked, offended, thinking naïvely that the items of gossip so cleverly planted in Punta del Este could have fabricated a lover for me in La Paloma.

"Then, do you have a lover?"

"Look, Humberto, I've had enough lovers so I can take a summer off without acquiring a reputation as a lesbian. I had no intention of looking for one in La Paloma; besides, why fool ourselves? The men around here are not shining examples of virility...."

"Or you're not a shining example of femininity."

"As you wish. But I am a grandmother and do not need lovers to keep me from being the victim of your slanders."

"I'm not the slanderer; it's *vox populi.*"

I wondered if I should slap him. No, better to explain ourselves, to try to keep on being civilized in the middle of nowhere.

"What charges have been brought against me in this witch hunt?"

"Socializing with social outcasts."

"Social outcasts according to whom?"

"Well...according to everybody: Belgians, French, Italians, Argentineans."

"I'm not at the United Nations. Talk to me in modest, human terms."

"It comes to the same thing. It just happens that we're international here."

"I'm not. I met Diana and made friends with her. Her cousin

is leaving tomorrow, and as I've already mentioned, she's quite an amusing woman. She says unexpected things, something I can't say about you and your League of Nations. What the heck does this have to do with lesbianism?"

"Nothing. But they have that reputation."

"And where does that reputation come from?"

"How should I know?"

"Don't be a bore, Humberto. It's also being said that people take drugs at The Magic Seashell, and we all know that's not true. But what would become of our simple, comfortable, restful holidays here if word got out that our greatest fun is eating mussels and drinking white wine? All the idiots cruising the roads the world over would come here as soon as it started warming up."

"You are one of them."

"I admit it, but I'm not bothering anybody. Leave Diana in peace along with the little old witch disguised as a good fairy. They have brought me more than you have."

"And Nino?"

"What do you mean, Nino?"

"Nothing...I thought...."

"Do you always believe all the nonsense which reaches your ears? You are the most believing person I've ever met. Why didn't you go into a monastery?"

I got in the car, started the engine, was about to accelerate madly, but Humberto took my hand and kept me there.

"Don't go away angry. You know how much I like you."

"Ah, yes, you're in a jealous rage because I didn't come to your tavern for four days."

"Five...five days, not four."

We both laughed.

"Don't worry about me. I still like men even if they may like me much less."

"Sorry if I didn't come up to your expectations."

"I adore you, Humberto...."

I drove off without hearing his reply.

This conversation left me feeling uncomfortable. I went to sleep after swearing to myself I would find out the truth about Diana the next day. If she was not a normal woman, her friendship was a nuisance. I accept pederasts because they don't involve me in their perverse behavior, but not lesbians. And that little old lady carrying sticks of dynamite under the shawl knit by her own skillful hands on spring evenings in the grape arbor....Fortunately, there's such a thing as sleep, and I managed to submerge myself in it like an expert swimmer in deep water.

February 3

Nickie is arriving. Her telegram has preceded her by a few hours. I'm going all out to arrange her room. The rest doesn't matter.

While I create space in the closet, put flowers on the dresser, and check the towels, I'm wondering if Nickie's marriage will be as sensible as Dolores'. I often think we are witnessing the phenomenon of a sexless generation. I would like to get to the causes, but it would be a long and difficult task, since statistics are laughable or require a whole lifetime of dedication. The fact is that on one of the few occasions when Dolores and I had a friendly talk, she reproached me for my generation and the next being made up of women prone to excess. We believed love to be an activity which, like art, is enough to fill up and even justify a life. For the women of Dolores' generation, it is an act. And for the men? It's the same, she said scornfully. Alejandra's explanation was somewhat similar: life is hard, they want to make a place for themselves, they aren't about to play at being romantic. They obey their limited passionate urges and maybe even force themselves a little, but there is an entire world which is out of their grasp. Our long Sunday afternoon naps would bore them to death. They prefer to go boating.

What subtle authors or frustrated mothers succeeded in making us into men and women who explored love as if it were the tombs of the pharaohs or the Parthenon, knowing it was a privilege which had been magnanimously offered and should be accepted with our last drop of blood? Of all this, we passed on to the young only the brutal and anti-aesthetic sensations of an act. They performed it as such. Of course, they don't deprive themselves of performing it, before or after marriage, whenever they have the urge. But they don't have the urge very often. A young husband no longer takes pride in giving his wife in a single day repeated demonstrations of his love. I know that Facundo will water ski, Nickie will brown herself in the sun like a slice of breakfast toast, but they will not shut themselves in their room, absorbed in that mystery which ruled our lives. Do you remember, Santiago, how I would nap more soundly than you, only to be interrupted by the urgency of your need? Do you remember the ice-cold cherries, the verses of Baudelaire, the hours outside of time? We at least did not lose our youth. All the rest, as Engracia says, only leaves behind in the long run the unmistakable taste of failure.

February 4, night

I went to say goodbye to Diana's cousin, courageously, facing the cross-eyed looks of the local residents. I told her I had just a few minutes because my youngest daughter was arriving with her husband and she was pregnant.

"How many months?" asked Engracia in a most tender, interested fashion.

"I don't know exactly. She was married October seventh, today is February second, it's probably three months," I replied conventionally.

"I didn't ask you when she got married," she said sweetly,"but how advanced her pregnancy is."

"But...I assumed...."

"How strange! A young woman like you assuming the same thing my grandmother would have assumed or your grandson would assume, that babies are born after weddings."

I stood there dumfounded.

Nickie arrived six months pregnant, and exactly as I had pictured her—an olive with a toothpick stuck through it. I couldn't go tell Engracia since she had already left; besides, it doesn't please me that other people are always right. Diana came to dinner and smiled at recalling the words of her cousin, whom she greatly admires.

I am besieged with problems today, but tomorrow or the day after I will let her know what's being said about her. Perhaps this story about pirates is simply a way of justifying her abnormal tendencies.

I'm dead on my feet. I will continue this tomorrow.

February 5

I'm wondering if Nickie used such an ignoble weapon to snare Facundo. If she did, I'll think a little less of her. They play at being liberated, and they use the methods of washerwomen to snare husbands.

February 6, late

I was abrupt with Nickie. I told her I wouldn't care if she showed up with an illegitimate child (what a lie) but if that was how she tried to snare Facundo I considered her a sort of prostitute, incapable of facing life and its responsibilities on her own.

She replied that she and Facundo had decided to dispense with all the pills etcetera and force his parents to speed up the wedding date. His parents knew, and I didn't! I didn't, because they didn't need me. What purpose did it serve to involve me? I wasn't going to present them with an apartment or a European honeymoon. I thought of Engracia, misunderstood, slandered, simply for speaking the truth.

Their apartment would be done early in March. Until then they would continue living in mine except for this stay in La Paloma. I couldn't say no.

Then we had a long talk about Alejandra and Dolores. It seems that among the three of them it had been decided I should hand over at least four out of every ten of my paintings. All artists' children make the mistake of undervaluing their parents' work; thus, when the *marchands* have put it on the market at fabulous prices, the children have nothing left but a few sketches. I pointed out that I live off these paintings. They replied they would rather make up the amount to me....I jumped to my feet. The little shits. My work is mine. I keep it or burn it or sell it cheap, but it's mine. If they want it, they can buy it from galleries. Offering me charity... me. I was overcome by anger. Nickie cried and declared that I didn't understand them, that I had never understood them, that I am a selfish, self-centered monster and should be psychoanalyzed. Facundo was consoling her and muttering, "You'll lose the baby." As if crying and getting angry are all it takes to lose a baby! I felt like shouting that most of the babies in the world are born amid the tears, reproaches, and scenes of their parents, despite pills, contraceptive devices, or doses of quinine. Nothing stops humanity's advance on the planet it has been assigned the burdensome task of ruling.

In the course of the conversation, I came to understand a great deal. The ruby was to be Alejandra's, the diamond Dolores's, the sapphire Nickie's. Alejandra preferred the Petorutti, Dolores needed the vermeil dishes, Alejandra the Picasso sketch—the other things had no value in the United States. The three of them, by the way, adored me. They could not forgive my indifference at the most crucial moments of their life. I was selfish and self-centered. I left without slamming the door, saying I had an engagement. I went to Diana's house.

I was the selfish one, I who asked nothing of them, I who simply hoped to spend four months painting and dreaming. They were adorable daughters. Each of us could count on about the same number of people who would say we were right. To argue or to make one point of view prevail was so useless that I chose to do the only sensible thing: take my yellow windbreaker and seek refuge among those who don't love me, who may never see me again, but who grant me the basic right to live my life as I please.

February 8

Diana's story has calmed me down. I told her everything lumped together, indiscriminately, not thinking about whether I was wounding her: Humberto's gossip, my daughters' silly ideas, my defenselessness. I spoke to her of you. She listened and then agreed to tell me things about her life which confirmed for her that the curse on the despotic slave trader had crossed the centuries like a trail of black ants marching through the woods.

"No," she said with a smile, "I'm not a lesbian, so you can feel at home here and not be exposed to my lascivious desires. I married, I became pregnant, I had an abortion so there would not be another condemned child. As most marriages turn out badly, ours knew vicissitudes and moments of estrangement. My husband, who was a simple man, kept on believing the abortion was to blame for everything. I could not explain the truth to him. Moreover, I still didn't know it. It took me twenty years to find out. I felt unsatisfied. I had affairs with no future. Some would last out of laziness or habit, but nothing trembled within me. I wasn't frigid, let me make that clear. My glands functioned sluggishly, as do glands with strong, primitive sensations but without that other emotion which comes from deep within the secret self from whence man comes without realizing it. I sought out young men, then old ones, pinning my hopes on the well-known Electra complex. Nothing significant moved within me. Appealing to my vanity, I sought out brilliant men. Nothing. I sought out men of the people, taking a chance on that simplicity which is a defect according to the well off, who speak of 'our inferiors.' The glands merely went on working totally unconcerned with my inward yearning. In any man's arms, I was alone. Like your gullible friend Humberto, I thought I was a lesbian; but everything in me proclaimed the opposite. I liked men, I scorned women. With them I felt bored, and physically...best not to talk about them. I knew that in this world there was a man waiting for me. He was there. At night, in deep sleep, I would sense that he lived. At dawn, I would see him vanish. To be honest, he did not have a well-defined face. It was a blurry silhouette, like that of the thief leaping over the garden wall by night. I knew or thought I knew that he was tall, slender, with a cat-like walk, a gentle smile, and immense tenderness."

"Aren't you going swimming today?" said a voice next to me. I was so engrossed in Diana's story that it startled me. There's something of the child in all of us. In me this vestige of infancy is expressed in my ability to detach myself from the real world and float away, defenseless, into the world of fantasy. Nino stood there—the gentle smile and slender build Diana had just described were his. Nino! Might it have been Nino? I don't know why I felt a renewed wave of anger, which struck my chest, then went crashing over Diana.

"Go on, go swimming. Sunbathing with dry skin is bad for you. I have pains in my joints, so I'll just stay here. The hot sand does me good."

Hypocrite. Soft-headed old lady, in love with a young fisherman or swimmer or café keeper, I didn't know what to call Nino. One thing I could be sure of—he was as young and handsome as a Greek demigod.

I followed him, went in the water beside him, and for a long while we swam in silence.

"What's bothering you?"

"Nothing. It's hard to swim and talk," I answered.

"I know that. But you usually say something, even if it's a cliché, like the water's cold or warm or...."

Idiot, he's decided that I utter clichés, me. Me, no less! But is there any *me* in the world who believes him or herself capable of uttering clichés? I must confess that in this domain I believe my *me* less likely to do so than most. By nature I am inclined to believe in my own brilliance.

I decided to take the bull by the horns: "What is there between you and Diana?"

"What?" The shocked tone didn't seem to be faked. "What

are you saying?"

"I'm saying, is there something between you and Diana?"

"That old witch. Do you think I'm crazy?"

Diana was three years older than I, but the certainty that Nino thought me much younger filled me with pride.

"She's not a witch, and she isn't old," I said, floating on my back, with Nino following my lead.

"But to me, she's not a woman."

"And to you, who is a woman?" I said with calculated, trite coquettishness, taking for granted a man-of-the-world reply. But Nino was not a man of the world.

"Every woman except her...how should I know...Sophia Loren, Brigitte Bardot...every one of them."

"They're not every woman," I said crossly. "They are the exceptional ones."

"Well, basically, all us men dream about the exceptional ones. With you women, it's probably the same."

"Yes...perhaps. But don't you know any real woman who has an effect on you?"

"Of course. All of them except for her."

What did that idiot mean by 'all of them'?

"My daughters, for example. Do you find them attractive?"

"I might have liked Nickie, but pregnant women reject me. That's natural. All the work has already been done."

What a lout, I thought, and resumed swimming furiously.

"Alejandra is attractive, but she seems rather neurotic; besides, I don't know why she believes that people who live in New York are so much more important than those of us who live in La Paloma. Doesn't that seem ridiculous to you?"

Nino was right in a way, but most of humanity has a rating scale for the geographic, just as it does for the social, the intellectual, and the financial. And even if Nino resists the idea, living in La Paloma is not a crowning achievement for anyone.

"That's not it," I said, floating again. "You didn't understand her very well. The truth is that by her own efforts she's made an outstanding career and what's more, whether we like it or not, New York is a world center."

"The center ought to be in oneself and not in a place," Nino said with good sense, "but Alejandra is an appealing girl. To me, Dolores is unbearable—silly, vain, empty, but it doesn't matter. From women like that come extraordinary men, like Alejo."

It pleases me when Alejandro is declared extraordinary. I firmly believe it, and though he may never end up amazing the world, no one will ever erase the miracle of his sad smile, his faraway, melancholy look.

"In short, all the girls in the world make a good impression on you," I said, faking cheerfulness. "I like that. It's the sign of a true man."

"Don't say dumb things."

I could barely stay afloat. Never had Nino spoken to me in that tone.

"I can't allow you to...."

"You're always allowing and not allowing as if the world depended on your desires and moved according your permission."

This time I forgot how to swim. I swallowed water, and Nino came close: "Lean on my shoulder if you're tired."

"I'm not tired; I'm in shock," I said, hanging on to his shoulder.

He began swimming slowly, and I let myself be carried along, like a fortunate drowning victim. I helped with slight movements of my legs, expert at gliding through the water.

"Nino, why do you say unpleasant things to me?"

"Because you don't allow me to say anything pleasant."

I kept quiet. No, no, I couldn't allow him to say what he wanted to say. No, no, I didn't come here in search of affairs but of scenery for my canvases and solitude to finish my work on Manet. No, no, no, a thousand times no.

We arrived back at the shore as silent as when we had left it.

"Thanks for your help. You saved my life."

He smiled.

"Shall I escort you to your umbrella?"

"No, thanks again."

Diana was still toasting herself as she had all morning, with that same monotonous symmetry. She knew nothing of the tides which had affected me while she was oiling her left arm, her left thigh, her left calf.

"Go on with your story," I said.

She replied, "I've been looking at my calendar. *Carnaval* is next week."

"Yes, it falls early this year."

Both of us grew quiet. The story had lost its spell, and it was not in our power to re-establish the vanished atmosphere.

We got up, we packed up our nomads' belongings and headed for Luigi's little house to drink chilled wine and eat clams and mussels.

February 9

Nickie and Facundo are quite energetic. They go to San Carlos to buy belts, wallets, attaché cases, and they come back fascinated. Another day they take in Rocha and find fake colonial lamps. Last night they went to Maldonado for dinner. They suggested I go back with them tomorrow for a *candombe*, a performance of traditional black dances, in El Portón de San Pedro.

"With real blacks?"

"Of course."

"Invite Diana. Those things fascinate her," I said.

"No...well, if you want her to come."

That afternoon Diana and I went out and strolled along the pier. It was cool, and for the first time since my arrival there were clouds in the sky. The gray sea diminished the landscape's offensively tropical appearance, which so wearied me. I had brought along my sketchbook and began making some notes. I drew while Diana once again took up the thread of her story. "Does this really interest you? If not, I'd rather keep quiet. All this is too serious to fall on indifferent ears."

"It really does interest me."

"As I told you, this man inhabited my days and my nights. Stupidly, I would look for him at cocktail parties and dinners. I would try to smell his odor (which I had often imagined) on my partner while we danced the tango cheek to cheek. It was not he, it was never he. I know perfectly well that a whole lifetime can pass by without the person meant for us ever crossing our path. I ended up accepting my defeat and decided to turn it into a triumph. An exceedingly rich man—much sought after by all my friends—had fallen madly in love with me. I asked for a divorce, and we set the date for our wedding. He had business interests all over the world. We decided to take a trip together while our papers were being put in order. I wanted to go to India or Japan. But important men can't allow themselves the luxury of travelling as tourists. He had to go to New York and Switzerland on business. I agreed.

"On a hot morning in late June, we stepped off the plane at La Guardia Airport. A man in a porter's uniform was carrying the bags. My heart skipped a beat: that man was he. *He*. Understand?"

"What bad luck," I said, "to find yourself forced to exchange a banker for a baggage carrier. Your heart played a dirty trick on you."

"It wasn't just that. Don't you understand? The man was black."

"Ouch!" I exclaimed, horrified.

"It's so odd. In principle, no one is racist. Everyone condemns racist crimes, no one believes in class differences, but as soon as something takes place like what happened to me, it becomes apparent that everyone believes in all forms of discrimination. They're all little Hitlers."

"Let's not exaggerate. But, then what...?"

"I didn't care if he was black," she said, looking me in the eye scornfully. "On the contrary, it made me proud. What I thought about was that I would never see him again, and I was devastated. But we exchanged looks, and while my future husband was going through customs, the man said to me: 'I am a trumpeter. Every night I play at a club called The Blackbird.'

"I'll spare you the details. Of course we went to The Blackbird that very night. All blacks looked alike to my banker, so he didn't recognize him. The world is full of bankers to whom all blacks look alike, all Chinese look alike, and all poor people look alike. And that's the kind of man I had landed. But I didn't put up with it. That very night I told him I didn't love him, that I would never be able to love him, and that I was going to change hotels. My resources wouldn't let me stay in his.

"He just didn't understand. He advised me to take various tranquilizers and so-called happy pills. But I already knew where my happiness lay. And I was determined to go seek it, win it, and hold on to it, whatever the price."

Diana grew silent again.

"And did you find it, did you hold on to it?" I asked, skeptical.

"We loved each other passionately for an eternity which lasted ten or twelve days. Then the racial struggle began—his, not mine. Lionel had one fault: he drank, and he didn't hold his liquor well. After three or four whiskeys he would say atrocious things about my pale skin, my white-woman smell, my lack of attractiveness: 'You people have lifeless skin. It doesn't shine. It's liking making love to a dust rag,' he would tell me. Then he would suddenly be sorry, would take me in his arms and ask my forgiveness: 'I hate whites,' he would confess, 'I hate them because they consider us inferiors; basically, we are still slaves. Can you swear to me that they never had a black slave in your family?'

"I would tremble: how could I, the descendant of a slave trafficker, swear to such a thing? But I swore to it. To keep him, I would have sworn to anything. To keep the magnificent ebony statue dreamed of night after night since adolescence, imagined and hoped for—inexcusably—in the middle of a meeting, during a diplomatic luncheon, at every moment, always.

"No one understands as I have understood ever since that time his ill will toward whites, his rejection of our lifeless skin. I would cling to the glints and flashes given off by *his* skin, which stretched so tight over that well-muscled body.

"When we were together, the phone would often ring. He usually pulled out the plug or let it ring. But once or twice he answered and I heard him making embarrassed excuses: 'I'm busy...leave me alone...."

"Many nights in my dreams I felt someone was trying to open the door. I thought I was suffering nightmares or hallucinations; besides, Lionel always fastened the bolt. One night we came back very late after drinking heavily. We collapsed on the sofa which served as his bed. He was caressing me and insulting me softly: 'colorless, odorless white girl...silly, pale creature...do you understand why I don't want to be with you? Where can I go with a white woman where they won't look at you as if you're depraved and at me as if I'm an opportunist? We're both traitors to our people.' I was sobbing and claiming that we would be happy together, even by ourselves. 'Humans weren't born to live in solitude. Or do you think I still yearn for the jungle and that you'd like to disappear into the swamps with me? I like people, I like jazz, and you do too. I like hamburgers, I like eating popcorn at the amusement park.' I kept insisting, begging. I didn't want to lose him. He went on whispering, 'I like cowboy movies and the silvery planes landing at La Guardia. I like my car, hemmed in between thousands of other cars on the road on Sunday night...and I like black women!' he ended up shouting in despair."

"I sobbed against his shoulder, and I was already beginning to doze off when the key, which on so many nights I thought I'd heard, actually did turn in the lock, and the door opened. I saw before me a black woman, very young, with straightened hair, her large mouth painted a pale pink that was almost white. She wore a white sweater and black skirt. Lionel sat up, absolutely terrified: 'How did you get in?'"

"With my key, like I always do."

"Of course she had tried night after night until that one, when he had forgotten to bolt the door. Everything moved very rapidly. It's an effort for me to reconstruct the scene. She stepped forward;

he realized what was happening. He sprang at her; I saw a steel blade flash; I saw blood flow; then, with fury, he struck her. I was searching for my clothes, which she had slashed with her knife. The door was half open, and some neighbors stuck their heads in. The black woman was shouting obscenities. Lionel was choking her to death, and right before my eyes, he desired her."

"The police arrived. I endured every humiliation a woman can endure. Lionel, overcome, was surrendering to the woman. The police encouraged him to reconcile with her, to ask her forgiveness, to apologize for his infidelity. They gave me sly looks. I was aware of being a sorry sight with my dress torn to ribbons and my eyes swollen with tears. These white men did not pardon my treason to the common cause. 'Women like you are to blame for all racial difficulties...you unsatisfied, depraved women. Blacks wouldn't be a problem if they weren't always meeting up with women like you.' And the litany droned on. Nothing mattered to me. I could only see in front of my fascinated, horrified eyes the indelible image which still pursues me, that of Lionel's erect member thrust again the white sweater worn by the victorious, panting young black woman.

"They went off together, arm in arm. I drank my humiliation down to the dregs. Before going back to the hotel I bought a daytime dress and put it on in the shop. I tried to kill myself. According to the police this is expected in such cases, and I was saved by the hotel detective who entered my room in time to call the hospital. They pumped my stomach—in short, the usual story."

Diana stopped talking, but her cheeks were tear-stained and suddenly her body shook in a convulsive sob as if this atrocious scenario had been played out just yesterday. I felt immense pity for her, and a little revulsion. I am not a racist, I must not be a racist, I said to myself. Her love is as natural as was my love for you. But something within me rejected the word "natural." And so, it's admissible, it's understandable. I must find something to say to her, a consoling word.

Impossible that I who can usually chatter away was as silent as a fish swimming in the sea. She began talking again, perhaps mistaking my confusion for a gesture of tactful understanding.

"Thanks for not becoming indignant. It's the first time I've told the story like this. I tried to write it, to turn it into a play, a film script, a short story, but nothing worked out. It is my own story, uniquely mine, and cannot be communicated. Then I undertook the task of relating my family history maybe just so that at the end there could appear this natural epilogue: this trick of fate, this curse transformed into a one-act comedy staged on the hard benches of a New York police station. All the ghosts from the stinking holds of my ancestor's ships must have felt avenged that night. And I, my God, why was I the one chosen across the centuries and generations to pay for the offenses of a slave traders whose sin can never be obliterated?"

"Has Engracia heard about this?"

"Yes, she is the only person besides you who knows this story. It didn't surprise her. Nothing surprises her. You've seen how coolly she explains the Oedipus complex."

"But that isn't the Oedipus complex. You're making a mistake."

"Who says it isn't? Freud said it and they all repeat it. The most important aspect of the Oedipus story, the strongest instinct there, was the killing of the parents. The rest was just added on, and not because he loved his mother. She was handed over to him by chance, the result of a victory. He had not seen her before. Therefore it wasn't love for her which made him a parricide. He killed his father only because of his encounter with him on the road. He was a gentle young man who would not have hurt a fly. At least this is what Engracia says."

"You two are fearsome," I said in spite of myself.

"Yes, I know that," she said. "At times just our passing by is enough to change the life of someone who gets near us."

I burst out laughing: "Don't boast. Our meeting will change nothing, I can swear to that."

"Are you sure?" she asked. And without knowing why, I

shuddered.

February 12

I didn't go see the *candombe*. Diana's tale shook me more than I could have imagined. Facundo and Nickie told me the performance was something quite unusual for South America. They are very young and don't know any other South American countries, but I didn't try to dampen their enthusiasm. Perhaps they are right. Alejandra has come to spend *Carnaval.* She arrived yesterday. The three of them go out a lot together. I'm profiting from this by recovering a certain measure of freedom. At least I don't have to wait on anybody. The house is dirty and cluttered; I can't even think of settling down to write my study of Manet; I would be afraid of losing my notes and mixing up my documents amidst the jumble of wet swimsuits, crumpled pants, sweaty sweaters, unmade beds, sheets nobody even runs an iron over, dirty glasses piled up, greasy plates, and smack in the middle of everything, María, for whom straightening up consists of a wide sweep of the vacuum cleaner over the tile floors of this house on the rocks, where there is never a speck of dust.

Sometimes I can't find a clean corner of the table to write this "shipboard diary," as I call it. Truthfully, I have been going through a bad spell since I heard Diana's story. The world has once again taken on an insipid taste. I am afraid of something, and I don't know what. It's a feeling of foreboding. Today I'm going to La Pedrera to sketch. I need to be alone. That's why I came, to say, "Enough!" to family and friends, to be able to devote myself at last to what I like doing. But this "Enough!" is always for tomorrow. I feel depressed.

February 14

I'm beginning to understand the source of my fears and my uneasiness. The day after tomorrow, as soon as Facundo, Nickie, and Alejandra are gone, I shall make an effort to get to my deeper self, to learn my truth with the same integrity with which Diana learned hers. But today they are all here. At this very moment Dolores, Iván and Alejo are arriving. I hear them get out of the car and ask María if I'm home. How could I not be? Does the Sistine Chapel or the Eiffel Tower move its location? Just let them come, these tourists. They will disappear the minute the place seems uncomfortable, or if a strike breaks out, or if the weather turns foul. Well, today they'll happen on a raging storm. If they aren't clever enough to reef the sail against the wind, the boat's going to tip over.

February 15

I had a most unpleasant argument with Diana. I told her that according to the way I see it, she was confusing sexual attraction and love. Love is something else. It can only be felt for someone whom one admires, as I admired you, or at least with an equal. Her experience was not love. I have never seen such eyes. They cut off my words as effectively as a slap. I think I said irreparable things, maybe things I want to say to myself but don't dare. Or perhaps what's responsible is this burden of aggressiveness that takes shape inside me when I devote myself to agreeing with my daughters totally and to avoiding any arguments with them—I, whose point of view in no way resembles that of any of them, except perhaps a touch of Alejandra's here and there. This constant control over my words, my opinions, even over my movements and gestures may have made me pour out on Diana that patience turned to irritability.

I am still thinking, however, that a passion like the one she recounted cannot be called love. The proof of that is the grotesque, obscene image engraved in Diana's memory: the black man desiring his black girl friend despite his hate, drunkenness, fatigue, and ancestral fear of scandal. If her story had not shocked me so, I would undoubtedly have recounted to her the story of our love. I'm grateful she has not made it possible for me to do so. If handled, a flower dried between the pages of a book turns to dust between the fingers. I don't even dare touch our memories. That's why I acted badly in giving her my unfavorable opinion about the emotion which so shattered her both when she experienced it and when she recalled it for my benefit. She had cut open her chest to reveal her heart, and I saw only the enormous member of a sexually excited black man. Now, between the two of us there was a clouded secret, a bad memory. She would give anything to be able to erase her words; I wish I could have felt more moved and less shocked.

As the morning ended, to relax the tension between us a little I was inspired to say to her that the most serious aspect of all this was the curse which had so tenaciously pursued her family. I wanted to find out more about her aunts and uncles and cousins. But she was wary now: "They were murdered, they committed suicide, they underwent voluntary castration, like me...one of my uncles, a vice consul who thought he was white, really was castrated, in an alley in Johannesburg, because he was taken for a black. There, the olfactory sense doesn't make mistakes. They smell black across all the generations. People said the attacker was crazy, a truly demented person, since he said over and over, paying no attention to what was obvious, 'he is black, he is black.' Our relative, the consul, didn't understand it at all. He couldn't understand it since he didn't know the truth. It never stopped surprising him that the criminal had shown no signs of insanity until that night. Do you understand now? I'm not a depraved white woman betraying her race, nor a tolerant and intelligent person capable of leaping over the barriers of racial discrimination. I'm a black woman. . . I'm black!" She is so fair and blonde (even lighter than I am) that her declaration seemed to be a fantasy. But thanks to that shout, I finally understand her. I understood that her love had been total and true, that she had found her haven, her truth, she who was an exile from her race, disguised by nature in a skin color which was not hers.

But these matters are difficult to understand. If people could really take them in, racism would not exist.

February 16

I'm fed up, fed up, fed up. I didn't come here to understand the ghosts and aberrations which fill Diana's hours or to listen to Engracia or to endure Humberto's pawing or to play the perfect mother and grandmother with my family around me. I came to work, to be myself, to encounter the unique and real me, not the reflection of others. And in nearly two long months I have succeeded only in sinking into a social atmosphere different from, yet no kinder than, my previous one. I will admit this one is a little more out of the ordinary. At least I don't see my closest enemies together, thick as thieves, after having heard them carry on about each other just the night before. I am subject to fewer pressures. People aren't putting me into some airtight category as they do in Buenos Aires and Punta del Este, but I'm not doing anything worthwhile. Just a few sketches, ten or fifteen pages on Manet's parents and early childhood. This has to end. I can't spend what remains of my life declaring I'm going to say, "Enough!" then always leaving it for tomorrow. I am the victim of this endless delay.

Today I did a lot of thinking. I have noticed that in vacation spots one's sense of purpose is easily lost since the people around one seem to have none and are having a wonderful time. Taking in the sun, swimming, eating mussels and drinking wine at the Magic Seashell—these seem to be the admitted and permitted goals of everyone around me, and mine too. Yet I know that with the first breath of autumn most of these people will pack up their shorts, swim suits, and flowered blouses, and will occupy the place in life which is theirs, just as the children will occupy their schoolroom desks. Rationally, I know this, but it's not enough to tighten my hold on life. Emotionally, intellectually, the emptiness around me seems total. Attempting to isolate myself so I can work is not only useless but is acquiring a touch of the ridiculous and pretentious. All that matters is a bronzed body, an aura of health and vitality.

Besides, there are too many women around here. On the weekend the husbands arrive, which depresses me. It sets the stage for my approaching old age, and it makes more acute the feeling which so tormented me when I first arrived: if I were a man, I would have an official place in the world, I would be somebody important, and they would be clamoring for me in some office. My colleagues and underlings would notice my absence. Nobody misses a woman. That's why a most curious phenomenon can be observed: women who when young appear cultured, with a penchant for art, literature, or philosophy, usually become dull as they age if they have not managed to turn these inclinations into a career. They have interested and amused powerful men and have resigned themselves to being simply rich and bored in their narrow, problem-free world. Many women who in my youth seemed silly now impress me with their good sense and experience. In the Latin woman, life experience replaces that quickness of mind which men keep and maintain by using it in their active lives. It may be, too, that a woman's brain grows tired earlier. In elementary school, the girls are ahead of the boys, and little by little they start lagging behind. This idea is bothering me. Last night I went over and over it in my head during the family dinner party which left me completely drained.

Alejandra was determined to show us there is absolutely no truth in the idea that American women know nothing about cooking except how to open cans. I attempted to restrain her, confessing for the umpteenth time that I consider the ability to open a can a superior attribute. For me it's the only unfathomable mystery of the culinary arts. Possibly we lack suitable tools, but opening cans is beyond my powers; on the other hand, a stuffed turkey or a balloon-like soufflé doesn't present me with the slightest difficulty. I suggested she open various cans of ingredients that I could provide for her. I don't know why she seemed offended. Her sisters backed her up. They wanted to see what kind of cook she was. All day we were her errand boys. Facundo and Nickie went to fetch wine plus a list of perishables we didn't have and which will rot here if I don't remember to throw them out before returning to the city. Dolores and Iván went to the port to buy mussels. I offered to go out with Alejo in search of bread. I had to beg María to come and wash the dishes, and I promised to pay her double for the extra hours. She was reluctant because she lives in

Rocha, but Iván offered to drive her home when she finished. And to think I came here to simplify my life! I thought nostalgically of my long dresses and my blouses as colorful as tropical birds, but I was determined to keep quiet. I knew Iván and Dolores would be returning to Punta del Este today, early. Tomorrow Nickie and Facundo are going to Buenos Aires. I will stay here two or three days alone with Alejandra to help her gather her strength before she once again falls into the arms of the conqueror Bob.

Alejo talks little but grips my hand firmly. I have the impression he expects something from me which I don't know how to give him. We both know we are quite fond of each other. It is a fact not worth discussing, just as between two people in love, but we have still not found the appropriate form of speech for our love. I make do with caramels, comic books, the only beach ball I could find in La Paloma. He uses that ineffable smile and those eyes which never leave mine. We are like two wild creatures deprived of language. Maybe he is as weary as I am of being surrounded with endless talk.

At the close of an exhausting day, after Alejandra's grumbling because we had forgotten the spices (nutmeg in particular) for her sauce, finally we all sat down at the table, reasonably well groomed. The meal was quite good, especially the mussels, almost as tasty as *chez* Luigi, and they didn't cost even twice as much. The chicken in white wine dried out a little because we were deep in heated discussion when María heedlessly poured all the wine left for basting and we were too excited to notice. When we did, we had drunk it up and there was no possibility of going out to fetch another bottle at that hour. We solved the problem by adding Scotch whiskey. Nobody had remembered about dessert, but it didn't matter, because we're usually satisfied with coffee, and Alejo resigned himself to chocolates. I calculated that for half the price and no bother we could have eaten at Luigi's Merry Mussel, but of course I was very careful not to say so. Actually, I didn't really care. What's important is that in a restaurant other people come in, provide distraction, approach, chatter, or say hello. At home basic problems are raised which no one has the power to solve.

Last night, after paying tribute to the exquisite qualities of the mussels, we got right into the subject of Papa. At the first word, I shuddered. I know that nothing irritates my daughters as much as the "egotism" of this grandfather determined to continue living in perfect health and harmony with a woman who loves him, both of them enjoying what life still has to offer. To my family, this behavior is almost monstrous. But how could I change the subject when Nickie had so much to tell? The four had been together in Paris, where Papa usually spends the harsh winter months. He had shown them photos of his little place in Portofino, and Nickie had brought some back with her.

"It's not fair," Dolores grumbled, "to be working oneself to death in Argentina, while he's living like a king."

"I believe he lives modestly, doesn't he, Nickie?" I asked.

"Well, as modestly as all that, no. They rent an apartment with two very comfortable rooms."

"And it's kept so hot, you roast," commented Facundo.

"In all cold countries houses are heated inside," I said. "It would be too much if at seventy-five Papa took it into his head to look for an unheated apartment. Besides, it would be hard to find one."

At that point, they all spoke up at once about some student friend living in Saint-Germain-des-Prés in servants' quarters. There you had to climb stairs. Papa had an elevator.

"Nor would it be wise for him to walk up five flights...."

They looked at me, enraged. Was I trying to defend him? "Well, nothing he does seems worthy of attack," I said in a low voice. And to silence them, I said, "I have heard Nadia cooks very well," adding with my sweetest smile, "almost as well as Alejandra," in order to placate at least one of my daughters.

"Not that well. The puff pastry came from the bakery...she said so herself. She did prepare the partridges, but they were brought by a friend of grandfather's who has a game preserve."

"I hope you're not suggesting she should also do the hunting herself."

"Nickie's not suggesting anything," Facundo said sharply. "She's just answering your questions. She didn't make the cheeses either, and they were delicious."

"It's a science knowing how to select the proper cheese in Paris."

"You're not going to convince us she's a genius."

"No, I don't think that. I'm just saying they live as it suits them, without bothering anybody. I wish all children could say that about their aged parents. All my friends are having insoluble problems with the old people in their families. Papa is the ideal."

"Yes, but everything is being spent," Iván said.

"Now, look, his father, my own grandfather, ate up his ranch in little slices, like a melon. But Papa is only spending his pension."

"Instead of an apartment in Portofino in her name, he could have his money in one of those funds which increases."

"Why are you so eager for it to increase? If I die you'll divide it up as fast as you can, and you'll each get your piddling little share, and if I live I plan to spend it all myself."

"Not one of us has ever asked you for anything," said Alejandra. "I'm earning my living, and I don't need help from anyone."

Nor do I, nor do I, said the others. But now the subject had been brought up, and they reminded me I had promised to give them my "French flag" when they came of age. And they already had. It is true I had promised them the three stones—the red, the white, and the blue—but that was when Santiago was alive and I had no financial difficulties. My present life is not that easy. A precious stone is a form of security against poverty. Next it was the dishes, the platters, the Sorolla, which I had always claimed I detested. At any rate, they're thinking that sooner or later these things will be theirs, and waiting is a bore.

"Grandfather has some Buffet sketches that are quite valuable and even a Picasso. You ought to go, in case he dies tomorrow and Nadia is left with everything...."

"But maybe they do belong to her."

"Ah, perhaps. They said the artists had given them to her. She's friends with many writers and painters. They have a Paul Eluard manuscript."

"The fact is no one lives on air, and none us could live the way he does."

"None of us was a career diplomat for forty years. He didn't live that way when he was young, either. He worked hard; it's time for him to rest."

I longed for Diana's hair-raising stories, Engracia's open and disinterested cynicism, even Humberto's constant state of half drunkenness and the impudence of Nino.

We ate the chicken and declared it was better like that, on the dry side, since there's nothing more unpleasant than raw chicken. I was searching for a hundred subjects to get us away from Papa. They couldn't stand his living in Europe although Nickie admitted he spent nine months in Portofino every year because it was cheaper. He had told her he was leading the life of an old sea dog, that he and Nadia rose at dawn and went to bed when it was barely dark. The two of them knew it was a miracle to have an easy old age free of stress, on the shores of the Mediterranean.

"She didn't say anything, but he admitted that at times he becomes a little bored and the days become long, especially in March and November. He says that at heart he's a sociable man, made for life in the great capitals."

"He's shameless!" said Dolores.

I had an urge to slap her.

"Of course," I said, "those months would be better spent in Rome, but since he can't allow himself that luxury, I think they're acting sensibly."

The discussion was going nowhere. I had a feeling there were things they had discussed among themselves which weren't being mentioned. They wanted my official reply on some object or other that Nickie and Dolores needed for their houses. Alejandra, more transparent, told me she had been wanting to go off to Europe. For many reasons, she needed to get far away from New York....

"Well, here you're certainly far from there," I interrupted.

"It's not the same. I need a complete change. I will confess that if you were to give me one of the jewels, I would rather sell it and take a trip, which I need as much as I need air."

"Me too," I said calmly.

A few moments of silence followed. Then we spoke of the coming birth of Nickie's child. I knew this subject would result in their arguing among themselves, and they would move away from that of me and Papa. To Dolores, Nickie's pregnancy was a scandalous matter. To Alejandra it was an act of cowardice: "I would never go into a marriage pregnant and be forced to spend the rest of my life thinking about how I'd trapped a man with the wiles of a washerwoman."

All hell broke loose. How dare you! A single woman can't talk. What do you know about these things? Facundo shouted he had insisted on using this form of coercion with his father who considered him too young and in no position to get married. If Nickie were expecting a child, Facundo's family couldn't refuse to help them.

With us, things never come to blows. Iván picked up Alejo, wrapped in a blanket. Dolores offered me a kiss. María followed them with that ever-present handbag (I never have found out what she carries back and forth in it), and the car set off for Rocha to continue on to Punta del Este.

I know they left disappointed. They had all counted heavily on this family dinner to make me cough up some of my possessions. I could hear them whispering to each other as they said goodbye.

I threw a coat over my shoulders and went out walking by myself, in the direction of Cabo Santa María. I carried a lantern to light the way. Never had I felt so harassed and at the same time so helpless. What did they want from me? Hadn't I done enough for them by not marrying you, by losing you forever when I refused to send them away to school? You didn't like children, least of all someone else's three daughters. We never spoke about it, but I knew. I brought them up, I educated them, I loved them, but in their eyes and words there's always the same reproach which I find hard to understand. I imagine that in civilizations to come there will be people especially trained to have children, and others will not have them. What have they given me besides those looks of reproach and their adorable presence? Not one of them asked if I was working, if I was happy or miserable, if the climate agreed with me or affected me adversely. My life interested them only in relation to theirs. Apparently they believed I stopped living and breathing or suffering and ailing as soon as I was out of sight.

I felt liking weeping on somebody's shoulder. A hand took hold of my arm. I screamed and turned the lantern toward my presumed attacker. It was Nino. His fingers gently dried a few tears of which I had been unaware.

"You know, Nino, I'd like to adopt you," I told him suddenly, addressing him familiarly, with *tú,* for the first time.

"Why don't you marry me instead?" he asked sweetly.

I looked at him as if he were a ghost. Then, reacting in a most unexpected way, I ran off toward the house without a word.

Marrying Nino—what sweet revenge! But what does Nino know of the Impressionists or Dylan Thomas? How could I stroll along the pier with him reciting Baudelaire, as I used to with you or with Santiago? What memories in common could we call up when, satisfied, we would lie on our backs and watch the smoke from our cigarettes create spirals in the air? Living...good heavens, why didn't they tell us back in our kindergarten days that it is such a difficult task?

February 18

I told Diana of Nino's proposal and asked her opinion. Naïvely, I thought she'd advise me to accept. I always forget that as soon as two women begin getting close they turn into close enemies. But maybe I'm misjudging Diana. Her words were sensible: "It was rather obvious...I think everybody but you could see it. But it's unacceptable."

I was angry: "Unacceptable! You've had a black lover who played the trombone and hauled suitcases. How can you consider my marrying Nino unacceptable?"

"Precisely because the same thing would happen to you. Or worse. I was guided by ancestral instinct, and you by a childish desire for revenge against your daughters. You like to picture Nino enjoying those dishes, those platters, those ivories your children are clamoring for, Nino giving you the strength to keep from surrendering to them, which you are likely to do sooner or later out of fatigue, weakness, or old age. The picture is appealing, but what will you do with Nino when your daughters aren't around? Embalm him until their next visit?"

"He is young and attractive. There are many things one can do with him without having to embalm him. "

"Assuming you like young, attractive men. I too thought Lionel should feel proud and happy because a white woman was dying of love for him. But he didn't like white women. I was a pretty thing, and my beauty left him cold. I was intelligent, and my intelligence annoyed him. It snatched him out of his world, and interplanetary travel was not his thing. He was fine in his little neighborhood, in his dark hide, in his humble life, with a woman who made love with her flesh and not with her head. To Nino, you signify something important, you give form to his hopes, which I know nothing about, but which perhaps fill his imagination. And he, to you, signifies nothing."

"He's so slim, so young...."

"You do carry on about youth! Some states exist only for those who notice them. Why do you have to like a young man?"

And, truthfully, a man like Nino never had any place in my dreams, even the most lustful. His attractiveness is so obvious that it leaves no food for my imagination. Besides—and why deny it—if I were as ardent and sensual as in my earlier days, I would not now be learning how insipid life can become.

The rest of the day I had little chance to think about Nino. I said goodbye to Nickie and Facundo and devoted myself to Alejandra as I had vowed I would. I was tempted to talk to her about Nino. What would I say? Luckily she hadn't the slightest interest in finding out what was passing through my head or my heart.

She showed me the latest letters from Bob, received in Buenos Aires. They didn't seem interesting. I am a monster, but her problems have stopped seeming important. She has her life ahead of her. She will meet other men and love again, and Bob will disappear into her memory; I, on the other hand, have reached the end of a road, and no other stretches out before me. It is as if I were at the edge of a precipice. If I lose my footing, I am annihilated. I have the impression that whatever I do, I will lose my footing.

All women my age like boys...not all do, no, but many. If I liked Nino, the world would take on new colors, and young people would accept my rejuvenation. They would not put me aside somewhere against my will, as if putting me in a concentration camp. I would not be their victim, nor would they be my victimizers. Could I be distancing myself from Nino because I'm self-destructive? Or because of class prejudice? I wonder if I'm just a sackful of outdated prejudices. If instead of being forty-nine, I'm seventy or a hundred. I deserve my daughters' covetousness and egotism. I deserve their indifference, their disregard for my problems, for my solitude, for my ambitions. An elderly lady has no right to nourish any such passions. If I were going through misery and cut off my ear like Van Gogh, I would have no age; but my painstaking research, my daily account keeping, my paintings as timid as my imagination, put me right in the midst of everything young people abhor. Except for my moderate complaining, I'm not at all bold. Nino would be a gesture of audacity. He would be the indisputable way of finally saying, "Enough!" to a world I reluctantly treat with respect because it has spent a long thirty years trying to tame me.

It's been two days since I've seen Nino. Maybe he was drunk that night or spoke in jest. I shouldn't have fled without finding out what was really going on. Now I am becoming increasingly disoriented.

I give thanks to Mother Nature for having let me know passion, that solitary, triumphal isle where two people land as gloriously as an astronaut landing on the moon. Aside from that, Earth is a poor planet without much to say for it. Thank you for having let me be madly young and malleable when we swam like two dolphins through the surf of the sheets. Thank you for my having belonged to a generation ignored, on a continent ignored, where we had more than enough time to love each other, to laugh and read poetry because those who held the power and the money never noticed us, and we were wise enough to know we were really coming out ahead. We were always short of money, but millionaires in time, and the pizzas and hot dogs we would eat afterwards always had a flavor my palate has never encountered again, even in the best dinners at Maxim's.

Everything has been stolen from us, everything, half of it kept by our parents' generation, the other half fought over by our children's generation; but they never realized that their condemning us to love was like condemning a martyr to Paradise.

It's true they left us perishable treasures which were to wither away with our youth. But the flavor of power and money grows insipid too. Anything human withers once it is in our possession. What lasts the longest is what is most fleeting: a love and the memories of it. It is the only asset which does not make us misers and which increases as we fritter it away, turning us into King Midas. Each caress produces gold, that gold which the young apprentices of today's sorcerers are hurrying to produce, but in vain. And, what's more, they are bored—their riots, the signs on their barricades say it, declare it, proclaim it! How pitiful! The poor young people of today! Their sin gave rise to their penance: they wanted to call attention to themselves, and they passed right by the miracle without seeing it. Their lives are as lusterless as mine now is.

February 20

Today Rolando returned from his excursion to Brazil. He was quite proud of having spent *Carnaval* in Río and asked if I had missed him. That type of question requires an affirmative answer, which I gave for the sake of good manners. Two hours later he left for Montevideo since he has to be in Buenos Aires tomorrow. Always full of non-essential obligations. More and more, I admire my father and I think affectionately of the phrase he never tires of repeating: "The cemeteries are full of indispensable men." The world goes on the same without them, but one must have unusual inner strength to face up to such a truth. I am afraid I am as lucid as Papa but less courageous.

For a minute I wanted to say: "Wait two days and we'll go together. I have nothing to do here." But I said exactly the opposite. I declared that Buenos Aires in February is uninhabitable, that here I had begun painting again, that my study of Manet was progressing and I would be able to turn it over to my publisher in early April as I had promised.

I showed him some paintings I had done while listening to Diana. He liked them, but he has no judgment in this sphere. I told him how annoying it is that since *Carnaval* La Paloma has turned into a sort of Greenwich Village where all visitors think themselves obliged to go about with a box of paints or a portfolio of drawings tucked under their arm. The truth is that for the last two or three weeks, in Humberto's tavern, in Luigi's straw hut, in the hotel, in houses, on the pier, I've seen over and over again La Tuna Island, the water tower, Andresito Park, and the same relentlessly blue sky, the same deep blue sea, the multicolored beach umbrellas, the stretches of golden sand. I did some sketches of the little crabs which scurry away among the pools. They were my first friends here, and I like their grayish-pink color amid the gray rocks, the opaque patches of wet sand, and the clear water of the pools.

My first friends...it's true that in a short time I've met many people. They've kept me company, they've told me their stories. The time has passed less slowly that I had at first feared. Yet I don't feel happy.

Alejandra went to Punta del Este with Freddy but left most of her clothes here. She declares she will be coming back. The night before last she went out with the Belgian diplomat. The wife stayed home because five of the little ones were running fevers. What a respite! The two youngest are barely walking, so for a few days they won't be laying waste our premises.

February 24

Nothing important. Alejandra is still in Punta del Este. I am depressed and once again sense how little weight my person carries on this earth. Maybe I should take out an ad: "Qualified woman—degree in Fine Arts, three international and two national prizes, speaks several languages, types with one finger—offers her services." For what? I could add that I have commercial skills and know how to cook. But even so I don't think there's anyone who would require my services. If I tell them I'm in despair they will give me the phone number of an association which tries to prevent suicide, so I can be cheered up; apparently their people are very good. Besides, to take out an ad, one must select the proper column since I shall be asked what it is I want to be: cook, bookkeeper, translator, or whether I want to sell my car, my apartment, my good china because I'm going away, my prize-winning paintings. If I answer that I want to be President of the Republic or Prime Minister, they will cart me off to the madhouse; besides, newspapers don't provide columns for requests of that kind. Come to think of it, newspapers are useless. They offer what no one wants—cooks who become enraged when one inquires timidly if they know how to cook: "In the houses I've worked in, they'd buy their desserts at the bakery." Then they hang up. If one inquires what salary they expect, they persist in asking how much we offer. Nobody offers the top wage right off. Timidly, we suggest a figure. They hang up. We come across ads printed inside big boxes, and they can be summarized as follows: "Needed, employee for rapid advancement; go-getter who speaks five languages, has fifteen years experience; top references from all places where no longer employed (for whatever reason). Those under twenty-one and over twenty-nine need not apply. Prepared to go abroad or remain at home office." In short, why go on? The perfect robot. I imagine that in time cybernetics will come up with those ideal executives who work twelve hours a day and who, like the president of a nation, take folders home to study on Saturday and Sunday. Laborers, on the other hand, want a four-day-a-week job and a six-hour day. I'm skipping that column because it doesn't interest me. I look at the craftsman column. Each listing gives a phone number. We call and are informed he's there once in a while. If we leave our number, he'll call when he's in. "Ah, you want a carpenter...to build a bookcase. I'm sorry, but I don't do bookcases." "You called the painter. Yes, but I can paint only when I finish this job. Now I'm painting the Wellington building. It has eighteen floors, thirty apartments per floor. When I'm done, I'll let you know." The locksmith doesn't have time to make keys, much less make a house call to open a door. If we are locked in, we ought to call the fire department. I suppose if a fire breaks out in the meantime, the locksmith will go put it out.

I toss the paper aside, out of my sight. I'm thinking this is the ideal place to throw oneself in the sea, to swallow a bottle of sleeping pills, to devote oneself to drink or drugs. It's a bad day. I'd better walk over to Diana's or visit Humberto. Since seeing the UFO, he's become a different person. He won't forgive us for not having seen it. Thanks to our shortsightedness, it's considered a fake. "But how in the world could you people not have seen it? It was there. It must have stayed three minutes...the park was crowded...you just didn't want to see it...or you're afraid. An order's been issued. They all want to make us believe these are space ships sent by the Russians. Filthy capitalists. This is what I get for living in a summer resort." He won't admit it's a test balloon.

Last night he scolded me at length about the UFO. It doesn't matter. I go outdoors. We'll see where my footsteps lead. The trouble with living our youth madly is that in the ripeness of age we are left with nought but ashes, like wood which burns up too quickly.

February 27

I don't feel like doing anything. There are hours of lucidity when one admits one doesn't have much to expect from life any more. To cheer me up, no doubt, the fortune teller who appeared at The Magic Seashell last night predicted an interplanetary being would visit me. Humberto was radiant. The chosen ones would now be two. The bar was overflowing with all the people who had arrived at the start of the month and whom I can't tell apart. Most of them leave this week. As soon as tomorrow, I hope. In out-of-the-way places I like solitude. There's a forced quality about the company here. It reminds me of groups of exiles I knew in Paris. They would always conspire frantically as a way of killing time. Here too we resemble comic opera conspirators. There's a kind of shared resentment over having chosen this place or because others have chosen it. They are making us lose the benefits of our originality. It's either them or us. There isn't room for everybody. Travel agencies offer on all five continents beaches swarming with tourists. Let them leave us this one as it is. Originality shared by many is no longer originality. All the guests feel somewhat guilty in each other's presence and seem obliged to expose to their neighbors the motives which brought them here. They defend themselves and explain their reasons. The tribunal halfheartedly absolves them. Human beings were born to choose, not to explain the motives for their choices. Some of their explanations are pitiful. I know they've come to La Paloma because it's cheaper, fancy clothes are unnecessary, and there are no rivalries among the adults nor any temptations for the children. But since all this involves truth, nobody says it.

February 28

Today the month ends. The heat continues. The fortune teller has enlivened the atmosphere for the moment. She told me Alejandra will marry this year. What do I care? I felt like shouting at her. But people don't shout such things. What I do care about is myself, I who exist for them only when I'm present. They never wonder what I do in the long days and months when I'm not with them, nor in each hour of each of those days, of each of those nights. Other people's hours are the real human mystery. How does each person fill those hours? Nobody wonders; however, between the moments we run into an acquaintance on the street or in a restaurant there are hours and hours he or she had to fill, perhaps ecstatically, perhaps despairingly, but most often tediously, in that gray uniform nothing, that opaque indoor world which contrasts with the brightly lit outdoors. Sun, much sun, there's always sun outdoors. It doesn't rain. Good heavens, will it never rain?

March 1

A catastrophic piece of news: Alejandra is marrying the Belgian diplomat. Sudden, isn't it? Don't be silly, Mama, it's been going on since I first came. And now what do I do in La Paloma? The wife is crying all day long, and the few remaining summer visitors are consoling her. No doubt the children will come and burn down my house. Now he has decided his home life was impossible because his wife never learned how to bring up children. Of course ever since he fell in love with Alejandra, everything is the wife's fault. In brief, tomorrow the diplomat takes his family to Buenos Aires; then he will put their affairs in order. This announcement delights me more than that of the marriage. Alejandra declares she will not leave her job at the UN since he will be transferred to the US, and she doesn't want to be like me, an idle woman who's lost her bearings. She tells me this in a critical tone. Yet she knows I've worked a lot and I've never stopped working. But this daughter of mine is among those who believe the world began with them. What we gave them before was chaos, and it's best not to mention it. Only when this chaos turns into total ruin, will they be able to rebuild and do useful work.

The fact is that she herself has momentarily sown chaos in the Belgian household. Apparently she has also cruelly disappointed Freddy because she swore she would marry him. Luckily Freddy is astute and prudent and has not broken up with his fiancée. It's quite a relief to know this generation is determined to redeem our errors. If they weren't, what would become of us?

March 2

The month began with a magnificent storm, the first I've been able to enjoy since my arrival. I adore the choppy sea and the gray tones of the water, clouds, and rocks. The surf is whiter, more cruel. The village seems more deserted under this heavy sky, and the cars—topped by luggage racks bursting with cases and bicycles—seem to be fleeing the anticipation of autumn. I have put on gray slacks, a sweater, and my hooded jacket. I walk happily, the wind hitting my face.

I enter The Magic Seashell. Humberto has lit a fire. He likes autumn and melancholy as much as I do. We talk of the Alejandra scandal. The Belgians have delayed their departure because three of the children are still running a fever and apparently the mother doesn't even have enough strength left to pack. I am angry with Alejandra. I'm sure she doesn't love this man. She simply wants to destroy a home which, in her mind, stands for Bob's home.

Nino peers in, hesitates, is about to enter, sees me, and goes on his way. My attitude has made him regress to his humble status as the son of a tavern keeper-fisherman. If I had accepted his proposal he would have thought himself a young Greek, a demi-god, king of the surf. I can't explain to him that he is a boy and I am an old woman. He doesn't believe it. He fears I think of him as an adventurer in pursuit of my money. I wonder why people of humble status believe those of a higher social class are necessarily rich?

Humberto offers me pencils and paper. We sketch silently.

After a while he asks, "You didn't really see the UFO either?"

I don't answer. We go on sketching, but now the spell is

broken. His friendship is lovely when he isn't harping on something.

"I will never see a UFO," I say after a while. "I've never seen a ghost, nor a mouse, nor anything that other people see. I've never had a premonition, nor a telepathic experience. No doubt I'm in the wrong generation. When creatures from other planets have settled on earth, I'll go on being unaware of them."

I get up. I go home. It's an ideal day for making progress on Manet.

March 3

What Alejandra wanted has come about, just as I had foreseen in spite of my lack of antennae: she wired Bob she was getting married. Bob wired back, telling her not to, that he was getting a divorce. The Belgian was sent packing by means of a hypocritical letter which I had the pleasant task of hand delivering. She even commissioned me to say she was giving him up as a result of my advice. She declares she loves him more than ever but does not wish to destroy his home. She mentions his sainted wife, his children, her remorse, and her confessor. Thanks to her I had to endure nearly having the door slammed in my face, then hearing insults until I explained the motive for my visit and handed them the letter. She embraced me, sobbing. He turned purple with rage. The redskins, believing I was an enemy chieftain, ruined my slacks with their wooden hatchets and left my cheek bruised with a rubber-tipped arrow.

Enough, enough, enough. Things can't go on like this. I'm going to the ends of the earth, without leaving an address. If I were a man, I would swear they are not my daughters, that I was deceived, but we women do not have that recourse.

March 4

Another telegram. In brief, after two months of doors opening and people coming in and out unannounced, the era of the bombshell news item has begun. Last night Nickie gave birth to a beautiful little girl weighing eight pounds, six ounces. Up to the last she lied to me for no reason. Does it make any difference whether it was three months or four months after hopping into bed with Facundo that she married him? But when it comes to delving into the twists and turns of filial lies, one guess is as good as another. She asks me to come and see her. For a long time I'm deep in thought, the telegram in my hand.

I reply that I've twisted my ankle and can't move for a few days. If I go now, I'll kill all three of my offspring. Dolores and Iván left today because they couldn't get a place on the car ferry for Sunday, and Alejandro's school begins Monday. They didn't come to say goodbye. According to Freddy, they are hurt because I didn't go to Punta del Este again. I am sorry. I would have liked to hug Alejo and meet Esmeralda. I dream of a future when science will be advanced enough to find a way of allowing us to have grandchildren without having had children.

But now, enough of family problems. I have almost a month left to think about myself, myself alone, and my work. I will paint some landscapes of La Paloma which the other summer visitors have not painted, all in tones of gray. The sun has come out again, but I have my sketches.

March 6

Today the owner of *La Barcaza* came to see me. I offered her a drink and we exchanged pleasantries. I wondered why she had come. I got the idea she wanted the house for Holy Week and I thought, relieved, that to be polite and proper I would have to leave before the date agreed upon. But I was wrong. She is offering to sell me the house. I looked at her in surprise. Why does she want to sell it? Her reasons are the usual ones, and valid. She bought the house when her children were small. She set it up according to her own tastes, decorating with reminders of the Greek islands where she had spent her childhood. Eight years later her husband died, and she doesn't like the solitude here, nor do her children. They prefer Mar del Plata. There one finds people, activity, scads of movie houses, theatre companies, a proper Casino—and not this baccarat hall where it's like playing a Sunday game of bingo—and stores, and clubs where the kids can dance. As an investment, a summer house is business at its worst. One keeps it for pleasure or one doesn't keep it. She would rather buy an apartment in Mar del Plata—the kids keep asking! All her friends go there.

Bored to death, I listened to this conversation I listen to often, patiently, when I'm in Buenos Aires. Yet, along with my lethargy, a little light was shining, which said to me, "Look, a part of your life has dematerialized here, and now there's something on the credit side." So as not to let her go away feeling hopeless, I promised I would think about it, and we said goodbye like good friends. Why explain to her I have neither the money nor the desire to buy the house? Her visit made me think of business, of obligations. I wondered if my cousin, who works at a notary's and takes care of my meager assets when I'm away, had remembered my recommendations, if she had collected this and paid that...I said to myself, why not go to Buenos Aires for two or three days? I shall meet Esmeralda and see Alejo in his brand-new uniform with the English school's coat of arms. I'll see Alejandra off. To go away, to go away as soon as possible. A compelling desire devours me. I go out to buy a bus ticket and book a flight from Punta del Este. Later I'll go on recounting these trivial thoughts if indeed I do return to this solitude which all of a sudden I can no longer endure.

March 12

"I came, I saw, I conquered." What a lot of history I have lived through in the course of a week! How many things have become clear to me!

I shall try to start at the beginning, which isn't as easy as one might think since our reactions don't obey the laws of time.

I spent a day in Punta del Este since I couldn't get a flight that same day, the sixth of March. I went to the rocks, where I met up with all my friends. In less than two hours there I learned some surprising things. The idiot of previous years had turned into this year's playboy. Women were fighting over him, and homeowners were proud to have him as their guest. He had spent two months going from one summer cottage to the next or staying in borrowed apartments without having to put out a centavo. All this had come about solely because he claimed a Brazilian medium had taught him to see into the future with sun-dried star fish which he would place over the eyes of his credulous friends before going into a trance. When they discover it was trickery, they will have forgotten what he really did foretell.

Then they told me that last year's pederast was this season's Don Juan. Two women came to blows over him at La Brava Beach in front of everyone. It's all they're talking about. Luckily, I told them, nothing of what happens in Punta del Este goes beyond its borders, which are enveloped in a mysterious halo of discretion and solidarity. Indeed, the magic of this place is the silence which falls over everything happening here. There is a sound barrier.

As if I were an old hermit getting a peek at fashionable life, I became absorbed in profound meditations on the fickleness of human judgments. They had just "discovered" a most entertaining woman or a charming man among those they'd been rubbing elbows with for the last fifteen or twenty years. No doubt next year these two would fall off their fragile pedestals, especially if instead of being available and supplying dramatic interest, they were in love, or bloated with happiness, or submerged in grief. The rules of the game are simple, but one has to be familiar with them and obey them. Human beings have moments of weariness which the world doesn't accept, least of all the fashionable world.

The next morning I boarded the plane and flew to Buenos Aires.

I had gone right into the midst of family life. Nickie and Facundo were now settled, not too well, in the new apartment furnished with the bare essentials. I found Esmeralda delightful. When her tiny hand gripped my little finger tightly, I was touched, forgetting that she would have gripped any one else's finger just like that or even a pencil offered in my place.

I don't wish to comment on the conversations eternally repeated in every family. But when I gave Nickie my strings of gold beads, I remembered that the bracelet with matching earrings I gave Dolores when Alejo was born had been turned into a large brooch since Dolores never wears bracelets. The first I've heard, I had told her sharply, noting the pearl bracelet on her wrist. But that was a gift from Iván; besides, it matched her necklaces. I had given Alejandra my turquoise beetles with the diamond eyes mounted in gold, and she confessed that in New York the costume jewelry is so pretty and the real thing brings such a good price that she sold the beetles to make the down payment on a second-hand car. I asked Nickie if she still had the flower of diamonds with the brilliant in the center, which I had given her for her marriage. It's a pity, but she lost it. She's lying. I know she sold it to go to Venice. "Besides," said Dolores finally, exasperated, "they aren't the crown jewels, are they? Basically, they were little things worth nothing." "No, nothing, had I kept the crown jewels," I replied, controlling my anger, "but to sell gems, I don't need you. I know how. I had to do it to pay for schools and shoes at times. But these are keepsakes from Mama. I would have liked my grandchildren to have them." With a dignified gesture, Nickie held out the necklaces: "If I must accept them under oath, take them away." Shrugging my shoulders, I left them for her. Are children supposed to know how much of the child there is still in their mother or father? Are they supposed to know how often I too thought of turning those family jewels into some stunning modern piece, but stupidly I thought of my daughters, as if I were a grandmother from a hundred years ago? Is each of them going to change her attitude one iota as a result of each of those little sacrifices, each of those humble gifts offered by parents who are not millionaires? As if children could forgive their parents for not being millionaires!

"Don't be mad, Mama," said Dolores, always the lead singer, not just because she was the oldest but because she had a clearer idea than the others of the value of objects. "But if you do want to give us something, give us your French flag once and for all." That was the name I'd given my three big stones: the sapphire, the brilliant-cut diamond, and the ruby. Silent, I looked at my daughters. I knew for certain that each of them had planned already how each stripe of my flag would end up. "They aren't of equal value," I said, to test how far they had gone into the matter. "That makes no difference," said Nickie. "I'm happy with the sapphire, which is the least valuable, if you'll give me your Baccarat crystal."

Silently, I looked at them. I stared at the gold beads to keep a tear from escaping. Santiago, do you remember how poor we were and how sorrowfully we would part so you could fulfill your duties as a young naval officer? Do you remember how lovingly you would take the girls in your arms when it was time to sail? I was a little jealous of them, especially Dolores, who from an early age tried to take possession of you. She strongly resembled you and was your favorite. In summer you would take her out in a little sailboat. In those days, I would get seasick because of a chronic ear infection, and I would stay on the beach playing with the two younger girls, a dull rage in my heart, as if you had gone sailing with a lover. After Alejandra was bigger, you took her along. Her presence between the two of you had a calming effect on me. It interrupted that intimacy which used to upset me.

On occasion, Santiago, the wailing of one of them would break into the music of our passionate love: "They do it on purpose," I would tell you, enraged. "They never cry when you're not here. They want your attention." Perhaps instinctively they wanted to keep us apart. You would never become impatient. "All babies cry," you would say...you would get up to rock them. When you came back to my arms, your skin no longer had the same odor, the mysterious odor of desire. You smelled of peepee, of spit-up milk or simply of baby sweat. "Go wash," I would order you angrily. I couldn't forgive them their determination to keep us apart like that. Yet I always kept my jealousy under control when it was a question of something important which could lead to important actions. How many times we had felt ourselves tempted to sell my "French flag" to go on a pleasure trip, just the two of us. But it didn't seem right to me; those jewels were supposed to be for the girls. And I was afraid of leaving them alone. And I used to put on last year's suit, carry three-year-old handbags, and wear sweaters I'd carefully washed myself to avoid cleaning bills, all so they could have new party dresses.

At times, Santiago, I've even thought we never would have betrayed each other if we hadn't had children. You wanted to leave the Navy in 1947, but they were so little. Seeking other work meant taking chances. I myself stopped you. You claimed you had great possibilities in a friend's shipyard—but what if things didn't work out? True, I could have helped you. I might have worked, but I hardly felt prepared, and I thought it my duty to be near them. I had been alone so often in my childhood, attending schools abroad while my parents moved around, that I thought only of giving them a firm and solid footing, a land they could love passionately because it was their own while their father sailed the seas under the flag which symbolized that land. On the two occasions I joined you in Europe I felt guilty, and I feared for them. I bought things only for them, except for those large maps which still cover almost every inch of the walls in what was our study.

At times, Santiago, I think that had it not been for them you would not be dead. You never would have sailed on that oil tanker if they had not paid you double. And now you would be retired, and we would be growing old together. We would have forgiven each other everything, in mutual, intelligent forgetfulness. They are your daughters, Santiago. That's why at this moment I say your name, and I turn to your memory instead of that of the other man, whom I loved perhaps more than I did you. You know that I usually address my words to him in my sad moments, foolishly, as if he were dead and could hear me, since I know the dead hear and see. And the living whom we have loved deeply also hear and see. With no warning they feel a profound uneasiness and know not whence it comes. It is the anguished call of someone remembering them.

Not only did my daughters keep me and Santiago apart at times, but also you and me, remember? I must leave early because of the kids. We can't go to the same places where Dolores goes dancing—that would be immoral. Don't call me at meal time, they're big girls now, they know what's going on. And to talk to each other late at night, I had to put the phone under the sheet and the feather pillow. Alejandra met you and from that day on I realized she saw only through your eyes. Maybe the desire to destroy Bob's home, the Belgian's, and God knows who else's, came from her being powerless to move you because she was only fourteen and you treated her like a child. Nickie asked about you on and off for a while. Then she forgot you, but she would have liked you to replace her father. Yet, it was they and that son of yours—so frail, so intelligent, who wanted to be a priest and whom you snatched away from the monastery as one snatches a child from the jaws of death—who separated us once and for all.

And all the above explains why I am now back here. During my four days in Buenos Aires I watched television eagerly, and it all seemed base, syrupy, sickening, measured out with a subhuman measure. I rushed to the movies every night. I was thirsting for the latest Oscar and Golden Lion winners, and the top films from Cannes, Venice, Berlin, and Karlovy Vary. Everything I'd missed this summer didn't end up weighing more heavily in the balance than the agonizing conversations, the squalid, dirty streets, the worried faces, the anxious gazes, the cursing drivers, the gossip, all the squalor of big city life. And so I had an old trunk brought down from the attic and filled it with books, the ones I can't do without. Then I wrote the owner of *La Barcaza*, who is vacationing in Mar del Plata, and made her an offer for the house. I took the French flag to a jeweler, accepted his appraisal, and decided to send a telegram to Mar del Plata to close the deal. Now I'm awaiting a reply. I feel calm. I think that twenty years from now Alejo and Esmeralda and other grandchildren to come will remember with affection the hours, days, or months they spend in this house. Their best childhood memories will be set here. Memories without the sour smell of school hallways and blotches of ink, memories with the smell of salt, the sea, algae, and skin giving off traces of iodine.

What would have been left them from the three colored stones? Long before they grew up, their mothers would have devoured those gems as they devoured the "trifles" I've given them up to now. Perhaps also they will learn here the value of silence, of friends who are signposts on the road, only that, friends without vanity, without last names, with memorable first names. Here they will learn that those who pass by are many, and those who stay in place are few. Passing by—they all pass by, like gypsies on the road. Some tell fortunes, others provide entertainment, the rest shake their tambourines, and those who stay in place watch them perform, shrugging their shoulders slightly, without scorn. Here, no one is scorned, and no one is judged. People are simply looked at as they pass by.

March 14

The owner of the house is coming the day after tomorrow, with her two children. The pretext is to talk over my offer, but I'm sure she's going to accept it. Before she arrives I want to see what effect my decision will have here.

March 15

Diana was busy packing when I gave her the news. She couldn't get over it. What? Me stay here all year round? But I'm crazy. It will be stupefying. No, since I'll be saving money, I can go to Europe for a month or two, and on my way there and back I'll stay in Buenos Aires for a week. Just long enough for a break during the worst of the winter. In the end she said dreamily that it wasn't a bad plan. But she didn't seem convinced. That doesn't matter. What does matter is finding out how the local residents will take it. If they are critical, I'll withdraw my offer and go away permanently. In a big city one can live amid a forest of criticism, but in a half-deserted village only warm affection can justify our presence.

While I head toward The Magic Seashell I'm thinking that nothing or no one will force me to spend here months which might be tedious for me. That is why I preferred to sell the coveted stones and not the Buenos Aires apartment. And maybe out of vengeance too, so they would stop coveting them. No, that's secondary. I'll put up with six months a year here, eight months perhaps. In that way, finally, late in life, a personality all my own will take shape. I will no longer be the echo of anyone, and I won't respect opinions I don't share just to stay in tune with the dinner-party chorus. I shall die knowing who I have been.

But first I think I shall go see whether my passing by their beaches was for the inhabitants pleasant, indifferent, or bothersome.

March 17

"At last, you appear!" Humberto shouted. "Where in the world have you been keeping yourself?

"I spent a few days in Buenos Aires."

"Buenos Aires, Buenos Aires. It seems that people can't live anywhere but, that the only human beings are there. Here we are mollusks and mussels for summer enjoyment, for killing time, aren't we?"

"I believe just the opposite. There people kill time, and here they let time kill them as it pleases."

"I don't know if that's a compliment for La Paloma or a criticism."

"It's a compliment, Humberto. Here the span of time given us for living exists. It *is*, like a rock. We have to accept it and wait for the sea to polish it. There we fear time, and that's why we kill it. The big cities are centers designed for killing time. Before, going to a lecture, a play, a film, was not a form of entertainment; it was my duty. I was supposed to be familiar with the world I happened to live in. Now I have the idea that it is repeating itself, but maybe I'm the one repeating myself."

"You never repeat yourself," he said softly. "On the contrary, you contradict yourself. Your inner restlessness appeals to me. There's something adolescent about it."

I burst out laughing: "Maybe maturity is a second adolescence. You can be sure that if I took it into my head to write my diary now—and I confess I am doing so—it would be rather like an adolescent's. Missing would be the man who always dominates the intimate diaries and novels of women in their prime. Sex is beginning to be a mystery for me again."

Abruptly, Humberto served up two whiskeys and handed me one: "Excuse me if I make up part of that mystery."

"I'm not explaining myself very well. The subject is risqué. I understand physical attraction less and affection, friendship, camaraderie more and more. Nor do I succeed in empathizing with my daughters' love life. Dolores' seems conventional, Alejandra's crazy and based on childhood traumas, and Nickie and Facundo's marriage is childish. I don't feel any shame in thinking of my daughters' or my father's sex life. Do you know why? *Because my flesh used to feel what theirs did.*"

"And now what's going on? Did it die?"

"Yes, a little."

"Excuse me if I don't go into mourning, but I don't believe it will be long before it comes back to life."

"Do you know, Humberto, that eight or ten months from now I'll be fifty? Even half a century ago that was the end of a human being's life. When I was born, I didn't have much chance of living longer than I have lived already. I am part of an unexpected collective miracle."

Humberto looked at me, intrigued. He came and sat next to me and added more to our glasses. Undoubtedly he wanted to make me talk: "I wonder what's going on with you. I don't know if you're euphoric or depressed, if you want to live or to die, if you're feeling the tediousness of life or a sudden blossoming."

I laughed again. He showed understanding. He was uttering phrases I had hoped to hear. We were not talking of third parties, we didn't need proper names to feed our conversation. Every two minutes Humberto would throw a few pine cones on the fire, one by one, and the crackling sound they made as they burst supplied a bewitched backdrop for our talk.

"I would like to be madly in love with you," he said softly.

"I would like to love you also or love someone like you, solitary and hospitable, a rare combination. Someone who, like you, would share my inclinations. Even though I don't like your painting at all."

"I'm not enthusiastic about yours either. I like your sketches and your interpretation of other painters' painting. I like your knowing what painting is."

"Do you know why I came to see you?"

"I never ask friends why they've come to see me. I am Uruguayan, Madam," he added, doffing an imaginary Cyrano de Bergerac hat, whose feather, also imaginary, brushed the tile floor, "and Uruguayans never leave a friend standing at the door. This is what our former President says again and again, quoting a saying of his mother's: 'Never tell a friend he can't come in and dine. It's a question of squeezing one more in at the table, of throwing a little more water in the stewpot, and there's always one more potato.'"

"Oh, I know that, and almost all those in my country who count politically had to learn it at one time whether they wanted to or not, and whatever their party. We owe friends a lot, and not all of us forget that."

"Yes, people do forget. Rich friends generally receive with indifference gifts from their humble friends . . . they smile and they say thanks, and then they put the present in a corner of the closet or give it to the maid."

"Well, if you'd allow me to say why I came to see you, you would not tell me that."

Humberto stared at me, surprised: "You're not going to tell me you've been mixed up in politics and you're in exile here!"

I laughed again. For a long time I hadn't laughed as light heartedly as I did that night. I had an idea I was bringing good news, and at the same time I was afraid to come right out with it, for fear of seeing it not well received

"Ghosts don't get mixed up in politics."

"Well, then?"

"I have a diabolical plan."

"Oh, oh," Humberto said. "I was afraid of that. Have another whiskey, and be bold and confess. What's his name?"

"La Paloma."

"Speak up."

"I'm staying in La Paloma."

"Yes, I already know that. Until after Easter. Holy Week falls early this year. It's a lovely time to be here."

"I'm staying until long after Holy Week."

His deeply tanned face, criss-crossed with wrinkles from too much sun, took on a glow. He hurriedly removed his glasses to let me see the cheerful look in his eyes: "What luck. You're extending your stay. Until when?"

"I'm staying in La Paloma."

"It can't be true!"

His eyes were no longer smiling, but moist. His hand took mine, and hastily he asked again: "Until when?"

I looked at him with infinite gratitude. Here was a man who was not my lover and undoubtedly would never again aspire to be. When, where, in what great city of the world would such a man smile at me that way, with that happiness—almost the beatitude of a believer before a holy image—because I had announced I would be living there?

"Do you think it's a silly idea?"

"I think it's too lovely to be true."

He raised my hand to his lips and kissed it. Then he let go: "I need another whiskey. No, even better, I'm going to open a bottle of French champagne to celebrate this divine madness."

I was expecting him to utter the word 'madness.' It was inevitable, but said like that, prefaced with the word 'divine,' its meaning was completely different.

"No, leave it for Easter Sunday."

"There will be more later for drinking with friends. This is just for the two of us."

He hurried over to the big refrigerator behind the counter, took out a bottle of Veuve Cliquot six years old, just the right age to have reached perfection, to belong to a good harvest, and not to have acquired the sherry-like taste of champagnes more than ten years old. He uncorked it. He filled two goblets and handed me one: "To divine madness," I said.

"To the most unexpected woman in the world and the most idiotic of men."

We drank to everything that popped into our heads. To seeing the UFO together on a winter night, to fishing out of the sea a green-haired siren with golden scales, to our friendship and to love—wherever it may come from, wherever it may want to go—and to all those who would be rejoicing with us tomorrow.

Later, even though we were rather tipsy, he asked for the details of my decision. I told him I had decided to buy *La Barcaza*, that maybe I'd use its large white living room for art exhibits or decorate my walls with huge frescos in my hours of spleen. All plans were allowed me. Everything except repeating my past as a supernumerary in cities filled with dried-up creatures.

He wanted to accompany me home so he could walk back by himself, "pondering his happiness." Thanks for that phrase, Humberto, and for everything else.

March 20

I had not had time to give Nino the news. He burst into my house when I was barely awake. I was on my fourth cup of tea, attempting to wash away the mixture of whiskey and champagne from the night before. He opened the door, then stood motionless on the threshold, unable to take another step.

"Is it true? Tell me if it's true?"

"Humberto told you?" Without explanation, we had gone back to addressing each other formally as *usted*.

"Yes, of course. And you know what made him the happiest?"

"No."

"That I didn't know it. He believed...well, sometimes people believe things...."

"I understand," I said with a smile.

I realized that, the first emotional moment over and his curiosity controlled so as not to dampen the happiness of our friendly evening, Humberto thought I was staying because of Nino, and that therefore Nino knew about my plans. Maybe he was afraid of being considered stupid and of having overdone his gratitude if my decision was based on slightly senile passion.

"I couldn't believe it," Nino continued. "I told him it had to be a joke, that you were bored here. Or that you had drunk too much. I couldn't believe it...I didn't dare believe it. You here... always...all year with us.... You'll come fishing sometime, won't you? We'll go...."

"Don't overdo it" I said, to calm him down. "It's true, I am buying the house, but I'm not a cripple yet. I plan to budge from time to time, to go to Punta del Este for a few days...."

"That doesn't matter. It's close by, and you'll be going in the summer."

"In winter I'll go to Buenos Aires for a few weeks...."

"Aha! But not too many...."

"To Montevideo maybe, to buy shoes."

"Why shoes?"

"Because I'm going to buy shoes." Shopping didn't seem to interest him, and I didn't feel like explaining the trivial reasons why I bought shoes in Montevideo.

"I'll be travelling to Europe."

"But then, when are you going to be in La Paloma?"

"Always...always, except for two or three months...or four...or not at all. Don't force me to make decisions."

His youth, his primitiveness, and that sort of dazzled love for me kept him from being as tactful as Humberto, who had strolled under all the world's skies and one day came to make his home here for reasons he has never revealed, but which were apparently rather gloomy ones. Now it terrifies him to go farther than San Carlos.

"I've seen it all, the Sphinx, the Parthenon, Red Square, Place de la Concorde, and all the piazzas and piazzetas of Italy. To keep seeing them, all I have to do is close my eyes. When I open them, I'd rather see the ocean or you." "Or see a UFO," I said with a laugh. And he didn't laugh. I repeated to Nino Humberto's very words: "I've seen it all, the Sphinx, the Parthenon...." But Nino didn't care about any of that. He wanted to be sure I was settling down in La Paloma once and for all. On top of that, my reasons seemed of no importance to him. The important thing was to keep me there, in his world, on his continent, on his own planet. His world consisted of his singing, and water was his element—just like a Venetian gondolier.

A few minutes after his son's departure, Luigi came to visit me for the first time. He passed on Doña María and Don Eleuterio's happiness over the news. I felt I was a precious acquisition.

March 22

We spent three days celebrating and two haggling over the price with the owner, who suddenly regretted selling what she now called her "residence." "I was so happy in this house. Believe me, it brings luck. The children had such fun here, and it was good, clean fun, and cheaper too—why not admit it? In Mar del Plata they stay up too late and dance so much they're losing a pound or two a day. Look at Baby Girl, how skinny she is. She's like a stalk of asparagus, and Boy is even worse. I've lost at roulette. At the beginning of the summer I won. You believe you're going to win all the time, but it's not like that. You don't learn your lesson."

I listened with infinite patience, but deep down I was afraid. I could not pay a peso more than the amount the jeweler had agreed upon for my sapphire, my brilliant-cut diamond, and my ruby. She went on stating reasons not to accept my price. "What if Uruguayan beach property goes up again, as it has in the last few years? Right now, it's low. Everyone tells me it's a bad time to sell. I could rent it to you for the winter."

"Oh, no!" I cried, angry.

The idea of living in a rented house has always been repugnant to me. I'll do it for a short time, but to live in the true sense of the word, it has to be under my own roof, where I can tear down walls, paint, add on, open windows, decorate with my frescoes up to the ceiling if I have a mind to, toss all tasteless items into the sea, change the name, or whatever else....

My forthright "no" took away her self-assurance and restored mine.

"I'm considering other houses," I said, lying without the slightest hesitation. "All of La Paloma is up for sale, and at lower prices. I was buying this one because you offered it, and buying any other seemed like an act of treachery. That's all. Besides I'm here already. But I can get moved out in three hours."

The children were fidgeting in their chairs. Baby Girl said, "For heavens' sake, Mama, don't make a big deal over a few pesos."

I noticed she exerted enormous influence over her mother. She was probably fifteen or sixteen but was trying to pass for thirty with her dark hair dyed blonde, her eyes made up as if she were an actress ready to step on stage, the calculated casual look of the pants tightly stretched over her rear end, and the man's shirt which was tied above her navel to reveal a large patch of flesh expertly tanned by the magnificent Mar del Plata climate.

"Baby Girl is right. Maybe if you let her pay some of it in installments, the lady...." ventured Boy, but I cut him off abruptly.

"The lady is not paying anything in installments because she doesn't have the income to do that," I said, my tone ironic. "I have given you my price, and it's nearly the same as what you, Madam, asked two weeks ago. I didn't want to bargain."

I knew it was going to be a difficult struggle. Uruguayans fear that poverty is just around the corner. Inhabitants of a small country with few resources, as soon as they have the chance to collect a sum of money without working too hard they grab hold as if it were a life preserver. Luckily, the children liked Mar del Plata. And the mother didn't seem to have enough authority to leave herself open to the bitter reproaches of her offspring. I couldn't see them returning to the isolated little white house of their childhood. Nothing corrupts like the hustle and bustle of life. I could hear Boy whispering in his sister's ear: "All the kids we know are there; here, we're dead."

We still haven't come to an agreement.

March 26

We are smack in the middle of tourist week. The descendants of the Aegean went off to Punta del Este while I reflect bitterly on how difficult it is to make a decision. There's always someone opposing our plans. My friends are frowning. Humberto offered to lend me the difference. I don't want to admit to him I could sell some other valuable things. I too fear life and always need to have something left to sell. I have lived through difficult, but not catastrophic, moments. That's why I often wonder in what former life I suffered hardships, hunger, cold, for how many centuries I've been dragging along this fear of not being able to pay for an operation or deal with some unforeseen necessity. Maybe all this simply arises from knowing I am among those ever-changing millions out of work they talk about in the newspapers. I am always conscious of having been relegated to the ranks of the unemployed.

March 29

Pages scribbled in Buenos Aires between March seventh and twelfth:

I found these pages I scribbled in Buenos Aires between March seventh and twelfth, and I'm inserting them here. They're giving me the strength to go on with my plan. I know I must distance myself in order to be close to my daughters.

Alejandra left in a state of happiness bordering on idiocy. A curious mixture at work in her: on the one hand, the fear-permeated joy of the woman who has conquered a reluctant man, and on the other, the triumphant look of the Nobel Prize winner. I don't know which is stronger in her, her love or her pride. At least now she has some secret weapons in her arsenal: her Río Plata love affairs. When Bob acts arrogant or unbearable, she will look at him with a touch of pity, thinking: "I too have deceived you, you silly creature. And I didn't find other men that repulsive, as you so naïvely believe." "Men can make love without being in love, but not women." Do they say that in all seriousness? How marvelous to believe oneself unceasingly adored everywhere, from the whore house to the marriage bed! I understand how such inspiring convictions make a man think of himself as king of the natural world.

Dolores is trying to make up for the security of her long, triumphant summer vacation by calling the furrier about her mink bolero and the cleaners about delivering her rugs. She needs them right after Holy Week. She is quite fussy and wants her house perfect. Yet I do sense she fears the tedious winter stretching out before her eyes like the pampas, the drawn-out, monotonous days of listening to Iván expound on his wise moves at the last Board of Directors' meeting, on the incompetence of his superiors and subordinates, on the disastrous state the business would be in if it weren't for him. And she? Iván thinks she too would like to feel superior and not put up with repeatedly strolling through the crowd at cocktail parties where they whisper in her ear that she gets prettier every day and that if it weren't for Iván...and silly as she is, she may even believe it, when the truth is that precisely because there is an Iván, others can pursue her and there's nothing compromising about it. I remember that two years ago one of her girl friends persuaded her to take up ceramics. When she started becoming enthusiastic, feeling dazzled as she lifted from the kiln little colored pots which gave some meaning, albeit fleeting, to her life, Iván looked at them scornfully, saying they would be good Christmas presents for the office boys, the elevator girl, and the maid. I think the future of both of them may depend on that statement, and Dolores will rely on it some day if she needs to find justification for one of her actions. Fortunately, at the moment, devotion to her social position keeps her from any moral lapses. And perhaps her sense of morality, the attraction which Iván holds for her, I don't know exactly. Nickie is already becoming bored. I think of her with affection and a sense of helplessness. She was not born for home and children. She hates all domestic tasks, and she looks at Esmeralda uncertainly. She wonders what this crying doll is doing in her life when she still thinks of herself as a child. She wants to be fussed over, to be the center of attention. She is at the height of her egocentrism, and Nature has played a dirty trick by turning her into a mother. Men are usually more courageous about confronting their shortcomings in relation to a certain way of life, while women in our circle in our country still consider marriage a triumph although it may be obvious even before they enter the Registry Office that they're heading for unavoidable disaster. I advised her to marry in Montevideo, in a country where divorce is possible, since she was too young and rather emotionally immature for her age. I told her they didn't know each other well and she didn't know what she wanted. She was annoyed with me, and Facundo said that was immoral advice which a mother should never have given. Ten or fifteen years from now they will be sorry they didn't follow my advice. Or much sooner.

Facundo now dresses properly, shaves, and smells of cologne. She still wears old blue jeans to show she has not turned into a matron, which is what she calls Dolores. She looks at Facundo as if he were a stranger. She is not resigned to losing the bearded bohemian who snatched her away from the bourgeois maternal home where there were fixed hours for meals, an arrangement which upset Facundo for some reason although I explained it had been made, not by me, but by our "domestic employee." That's what I had to call the maid in front of him so as not to offend his suspect dream of social equality. He has undergone a transformation, and Nickie is still the same but more untamed than ever. She is struggling as if behind bars. My house was not really a prison, but this is, and it's forever. Evidence of her suffering is the way she screamed yesterday: "I can't stand that infant's screaming another minute! When Alejo was a baby, he never cried. I don't know why I had to have a child who fusses all the time."

"You're in a state of nerves," I said stupidly.

"You know perfectly well I get nervous easily. When I was little, you wanted to have me psychoanalyzed, and your doctor told you it was a silly idea, that ninety-nine percent of the time it's the parents who need psychoanalysis."

"All that was still a little backward."

"Well, just the same you should have done it. I know I'm always going to be dissatisfied. Maybe I've inherited your neuroticism."

"Aha!"

I have never heard any of my daughters say they have inherited any of my balanced qualities, but they all blame me for having inherited some defect or other: my neuroticism, the tendency to choke on my food, my.... Why go on? I don't find myself that detestable.

But this little girl who's lost her bearings upsets me. I can do nothing for her. I did everything I could. I made her get her basic degree, then I encouraged her to study law at the university. She endured it until the second year. When she feels completely lost, she will take up her studies again.

"I complain for no good reason," she told me defiantly. "I have everything."

What is everything, Nickie? Shelter, food, clean clothes. You have nothing if you don't have yourself, if you don't know yourself or can't put up with yourself, if you were wrong to marry Facundo, if being a mother is not your calling. You do not have everything; on the contrary, you lack everything, and Esmeralda and the Argentinean Registry Office will keep you from wiping the slate clean and starting over. Now it's for you to try on your own to encounter yourself and reach an understanding with that Nickie whom I barely know and you don't know at all.

If you couldn't stay in Europe, maybe the trip was a mistake. I think there you encountered yourself. In New York, Alejandra learned that work is more than just a word and vented her anger on women who didn't have to work, searching desperately for a man whose arm she could cling to. Similarly, you, away from home, became acquainted with a world of young people who group themselves into fearsome legions and are ready to pay the heavy price exacted for encountering oneself.

I would like to help you, but my being here at your side now will submerge you even deeper into your role of housewife surrounded by family, where you are drowning. In the future you will seek me, and you will find me. After all, the only mothers really doing their job are those who can be found when one is in despair after mistakes and failures. These are the mothers who provide shelter for their children; the others seek shelter in their children. I always left you free within yourselves, as free as birds. I tried to exert influence without pressuring you. Now you won't forgive me for that. But you would not be daughters if you forgave.

"I like you in blue jeans," I told her. "You're not giving in, you're not playing the grown-up lady. You still seem like a little girl, and when your friends come visiting with little gowns and baby bibs, it reminds me of when you used to play house."

She laughs, a little more relaxed.

"And maybe this winter, when you have more free time, you can go back to the university," I venture.

"Maybe," she concedes.

Her meekness reassures me and at the same time worries me. I don't know what I want more from them, submission or rebellion. As I go to confirm my flight, I think about these three women. A little of everything will happen to them, just like everybody else. They might divorce, become widowed, or lose a child. One of them might die young. They might achieve success in some unforeseen way, remarry, go live in India or a city in the Argentinean interior, or in Paris or Rome. Their husbands might leave them, Facundo's father or Iván's might be ruined, either husband might grow tired of the daily work routine. Everything happens in the course of most lives. In some lives nothing happens, but without being clairvoyant

I see ahead for my daughters the star of unstable, embattled existences. I hope I can always be there for them the way I always stood at the landing when they were little girls and one of them would tumble down the steps. I was always a net and a parachute. They don't know about that and would know only had I not been there.

What I can blame myself for and what they unconsciously blame me for is having made them too attractive, feminine, and contradictory, drawn toward men and always seeking, like any successful woman, a way to conquer them and make them pliant, a way to submit and take possession. Sometimes I catch myself dreaming of the peaceful life of mothers with daughters who grow fat and shapeless in the flower of youth, daughters whose near-sightedness—unlike most people's—worsens instead of improving over the years. Such daughters are not their mothers' rivals, but their protectors, because amid such mistreatment by nature they have come up with the bright idea of founding a secret society, one of those freemasonries which take in ugly women just as three centuries ago the convent would take them under its roof. They provide mutual praise, they make sensible speeches, they believe they are doing constructive work, and perhaps they are, and while they're at it (to use an old slang expression), they obtain from governments and organizations what pretty women get thanks to men: trips, free lodging, silver in the form of cups and gold in the form of medals instead of the various objects of those same metals which fall into the hands of good-looking women.

My daughters are appealing and decidedly unbearable, and that is why I'm confident they will always find men who will put up with them. Otherwise, *I* shall have to put up with them, which is not nearly as fair, since I have no desire to enjoy their charms. For the moment I've had my fill of being maternal. I hope there's a direct flight scheduled for tomorrow!

March 30

The owner has telegraphed me from Punta del Este. They

must have told her there that "it's a down market, and you shouldn't hold out too long," in the usual language of real estate agents. She is giving in, but she is taking the furniture; actually, she is clarifying her terms: "as I offered it, unfurnished." Ouch! I was not expecting this low blow. In reality the furnishings are so ugly she ought to be paid a bonus for taking them away, but how am I going to manage to sleep without a bed, to eat without a table, to write without a chair?

Tonight there is a "family council." Humberto has gathered friends together to seek a solution for my problem. But already hope has returned to our hearts.

April 5

It was too hectic a week for writing; besides, as I said a few days ago, it's impossible to write without a table or chair. For a slight increase in price, the seller left me a mattress. Now I am the mistress of *La Barcaza.* We celebrated Easter at The Magic Seashell with three more bottles of perfect champagne, the caviar Rolando had bought on the boat, mussels furnished by Luigi and Nino, and a pile of canned goods brought by Diana, who made a surprise visit to spend Holy Week here. She couldn't believe I had stuck to my decision.

Today I'm going to Maldonado with Humberto and Diana to buy some wicker furniture and an iron bed the blacksmith owes Humberto in exchange for three of his paintings. I have a wicker chair, an iron table with a marvelous top made of mosaic tiles, the bed which Humberto "loaned" me, because I forbade him to use the word "gift," and several stools brought by Nino. There will be others later, next season, but for now we can fill in with these, he explains. Adorable Nino. Humberto also brought me a leather pirate's chest with an embossed bronze coat of arms and a heavy lock which doesn't work. It will do as a dresser. I am marvelously set up. We have all winter to paint rattan and wood. We all firmly believe it will be the prettiest house in the place.

April 10

I have so much to do I can't keep writing the diary of an idle vacationer. Nino arrived a while ago with the boards we'll be using to put together a bookcase. My old trunk has already been painted white, with red and green decorations. The books are on the floor. We've had many arguments with Humberto and Diana over what colors to use. The chest need not be touched since it's already so pretty. Luigi has brought me seahorses and some colored balls the waves have brought here from Oriental seas, where Japanese fishermen use them to ply their trade. We are intoxicated with decorating inspiration. Diana says she will stay on a few days to help. I do believe this is the first time she's enjoyed herself outside of bed.

A while ago, on his way out to fetch the hammer and nails we needed, Nino turned around at the door, asking me pointblank: "It's true you're staying? It's not a whim, your decision is final?"

"As final as any human decision," I said, smiling.

My smile cast a cloud of melancholy over his face. But he smiled also.

In a low voice he said, "Sometimes people do change their minds. Not just about a house or a place, but about people, about love. Even a decision about love might not be final."

And while there crept into my voice and my eyes a little spirit of mockery (whether directed toward him or toward myself I don't know), I repeated softly, "as final as any human decision."

May 2

I put this diary aside because it lost its significance. The outlandish characters who people summer vacations aren't showing up any more. Everything has fallen into place, calmly, sleepily. I myself feel drowsy. I wonder what I'm doing in the role of little Red Riding-Hood with a market basket hanging on my arm or my bicycle, with bottles clinking on the floor of my car. Will I have to reach the humiliating conclusion which nobody wants to reach, that I am just like everybody else? That everybody is just like everybody else? That in summer I like to do what vacationers do and that in winter I like to shake out the mothballs and take the furs out of cold storage? No. It isn't that either. Good heavens, how little I know myself. As soon as I am alone, I wonder who this stranger is.

The house is turning out to be perfect, but the woman who lives here is not really me. I am a flawless actress in the middle of a set endlessly discussed by affectionate stage designers. What am I, who am I without my past; without my burden of attachments and conflicts; without that city where I can feel my way like a blind man in his quarters; without that nearly half century of experiences, good and bad, passionate and tedious, intense and superficial; without the witnesses to those experiences; without known and unknown friends and known and unknown enemies? What am I without my own reflection embellished or distorted by the will of others, by mirages and legends?

Does there exist an adult human being who is something more or something less than that gallery of mirrors which reflect so many ghosts alongside his or her own image? Does a rose exist without a rosebush, or a rosebush without a plot of ground? Does there exist an unanchored boat, no matter how vagabond, that is not always heading toward some port? Is my port this vast beach, this serene, solitary place, so different from my own vagabond soul, as uneven as a goat path? I don't know. *La Barcaza* is increasingly homelike and comfortable. My friends take care of me as if I were a mental patient who might at any moment flee the asylum. Their hands support me as if I were a valuable crystal amphora. But, unwittingly, at times they pester me, and at times they are unaware of my long hours of solitude. It is true that I have finished my study of Manet, and now I'm writing on Van Gogh. There'll always be someone in the world writing on Van Gogh or Poe; lives of triumph and disaster are tantalizing. They allow us to hope for everything from the future, to resign ourselves to the present, and to rebel against injustice. They allow us to admire genius without envying it. Besides, people understand genius better if it is in pain. A wound doesn't need explaining, and it bleeds without help from anyone.

May 3

Today I painted all morning. Every day I have less talent and less desire to pretend I do, frantically reaching for the brass ring. I know the formulas for success by heart, but, like mushroom dishes, they don't agree with me.

May 7

Resuming this diary began to cheer me up, but my life is marked by the unexpected. Since I'm rushed, I'll summarize: they bring me an air express letter. I'm invited to the Venice Biennale and then on to Athens to do posters for the Piraeus Theater Company, which will be coming to Buenos Aires. I raise my eyes. Nino is perched on a ledge weatherstripping the windows to keep out the cold which begins to be felt in earnest. Humberto, triumphant, is putting the finishing touches on a sketch of the UFO which we really did see the night before last from The Magic Seashell. We've both tried to capture it with our brushes.

"Stop, stop," I say in a shaky voice, "There's no rush."

All eyes converge on me, even Diana's. She is lining my cupboard with polka-dotted shelf paper.

"There's time," I add, trying to keep down the enthusiasm vibrating in my voice.

I hold out the letter. Diana, the closest, takes it. Humberto and Nino grab it from her. I look at them with the humble eyes of a dog which has just done something naughty. I know that by leaving I betray them. I can't be trusted. But I am going to return. I will be here early in September. Humberto and Nino can't understand it. They are both sedentary—one by a vocation which came late, the other by birth. My betrayal is horrifying, and one thing is quite clear: I can't be relied on. All nomads are suspect, traitors to their group, their family, their country. No one excuses them. They provoke envy, criticism, indignation. I am going away. I'm deserting those who have never deserted me, who have made *La Barcaza* this retreat where I'd like to live and to die...but I can't. How can I give up seeing the Parthenon in moonlight again, maybe receiving a prize in Venice? How can I give up new faces, new voices which will enrich my destiny?

Finally, they blow up. I promised to say, "Enough!" and I'm letting myself be pulled away by the first temptation, no doubt intimidated by the long autumn afternoons. I'll never be more than a leaf in the wind, I'll never be able to hold onto anyone's affection, nor be a member of a group. No, never, I whisper, overwhelmed. They persist: never will I learn to say, "Enough!" Ah, that's not so! I'm not obliged to say it today. Fate usually allows more time. I swear that after this trip it will be over and done with, and the next day I'll say, "Enough!" no matter what happens....

But Nino and Humberto have already departed, slamming the door behind them. I stare at the wood they have so lovingly polished and painted. Those two! To think they dare blame me for my instability, as if I were not the only one with a right to assign responsibility. They don't realize I should abhor them for not having found the only magic formula which stops and holds a woman: love. There is not a single look which expresses enough love for me to keep me quietly in one corner of the world. Not from my daughters nor from either of you. That's why I cannot bring my wandering phase to an end. I could not even forgive you, my one great love, for not having tried to hold me. Humberto—you who know as I do that there is nothing for us in the technicolor mirages of a world of which we merely skim the surface—why did you not manage to love me nor to make me love you? We might have had an intense, warm world of our own, one of those worlds so miraculous they do not even awaken envy. And you, Nino...? Ah, why, why does no one find a valid reason for saying to me, "Do not go away" ? How I hate them for that.

Diana takes me out of my self-absorption by tapping me on the shoulder. She has taken my lightweight luggage from the closet and points to it, smiling. I smile and I have an idea she has guessed at my conscious defeat underscored by a series of successes. I start packing. I am already far, far away. My assigning blame is as unfair as is theirs. Fate inexorably clears a way for us without paying heed to our childish personal plans.

I don't even see the risky, choppy Atlantic now, but the Aegean Sea and the narrow canals of Venice. All the rivers and oceans of the world are criss-crossing in my head as in a globe of the earth. The Mediterranean, the Moldau, the Seine, the Tiber, the Genil...they are all singing in their various tongues. In my heart a sweet nostalgia for La Paloma is growing, and the village takes on the form of the bird whose name it bears: a dove, its feathers stained with drops of blood from the wound I have opened. Together the dove and I will come back to life next spring, when I shall have the strength of character to say at last, "Enough!" without demanding help from others. An ironic voice is whispering inside me: will it always be tomorrow, then? All right, what if instead of today it is tomorrow? But as sure as there is a God in Heaven, tomorrow I will say, "Enough!"